Anthony

BENTLEY LEGACY BOOK 5

KATHI S. BARTON

This is a work of fiction. Names, characters, places, and incidents are products of the author's imagination or are used fictitiously and are not to be construed as real. Any resemblance to actual events, locations, organizations, or persons, living or dead, is entirely coincidental.

World Castle Publishing, LLC
Pensacola, Florida
Copyright © Kathi S. Barton 2016
Paperback ISBN: 9781629895741
eBook ISBN: 9781629895758
First Edition World Castle Publishing, LLC, October 31, 2016
http://www.worldcastlepublishing.com

Licensing Notes
Cover: Karen Fuller
Editor: Maxine Bringenberg

CHAPTER 1

Coleen signed her name to the last page and closed the thick file that had been handed to her. The man across from her, Harry Mercer, hadn't been a bastard; he could have been, but he was nice to her. She thought that might have hurt most of all. When he asked her if she had any questions, she wanted to ask him why her, but she knew he'd have no more answers to that than she did.

"No. I'm going to go live with my grandma, try to get my life together and get a job. They're taking most of my money, so I'll have to live very frugally until I win the lottery." She meant it as a joke but it failed miserably, much as her life had. "How can I make arrangements to pay you back?"

"I told you, I've made an arrangement with the firm I work for, and this will be a pro-bono case. You have enough to worry about right now, Ms. Greer. And don't forget, you have to have whomever you work for contact us so that we can make arrangements for the money to come here. And then we'll disperse the payments that we've lined out for you. You'll be all right. How about we go and celebrate that this is going to be behind you soon?" She told him she just wanted to get out of town. "When do you leave? Not right away, I hope."

"Today. I've had to sell my house and things, so I don't have anything left here. Grandma has room for me for the time being, and she'll need help with my brother's little girl." She smiled when she thought of the little tyke. "She's a handful, Grandma said. Sweet, but a little energetic for a seventy-year-old to handle."

"I bet she is." Coleen realized that she was taking up this man's time, and he'd given her a lot over the last few weeks. "Coleen, are you going to be all right? I know that you didn't cause any of this, but the law is the law. I think we're lucky that I was handed this information rather than some other firm. They might have taken you to the cleaners. If you have any questions now or later, just call me. No other lawyer is going to be able to answer them like I can."

"I understand. I thought we were divorced. Apparently, I should have looked better at the paperwork he sent back to me." The man nodded and smiled. She didn't think this was funny, but he might have just been thinking how sad she was. "Thank you so much. You've been very kind. I'm not…it's been a long time since someone has gone out of their way to be nice to me."

As she left the big building, she did wonder what she was going to do now. Her car was loaded with her entire life. And she had just enough money in her purse to pay for gas and as little food as she could eat to get to her next landing spot. Micky

Anthony

hadn't been a bastard when they'd been married, but this had simply come out of nowhere. The man had been a fruitcake, sure, but she'd never have thought him to have had the brains to have pulled this shit. And now that he was dead, she couldn't go and find out what he'd been thinking.

No one had said a word about the divorce paperwork. She hadn't thought a thing about it until she'd been summoned to the courthouse under the guise of being the only living relative to one Mick Greer. When she'd produced copies of the divorce papers that she'd filed to show that she had nothing to do with his debt, they had produced the paperwork that had been filed at the courthouse. It had been fake; nothing about it even made sense. It looked as if Micky had rambled on for several pages about a baseball game that he'd bet on, then about the house that he'd wanted to buy with the money had he won. No one had checked it at the courthouse when she'd taken it to be filed, and she was still legally married. For as much as she found that hard to believe, it was the debt that he'd run up in her name that had floored her.

She had no cell phone...the service had been cut off days ago. There wasn't any way for her to call her Grandma and let her know she was coming either. Her money would have to last her the week it would take her to drive there. And calling her would be too costly. So Coleen got into her car and started her trip.

Why she had married Micky was a mystery to her. She had been working in Vegas at the time as a dealer, trying to save up her money, and had woken up not only married to the man who had bothered her all night, but also in a house that wasn't

7

hers...as well as naked. When she tried to get away from him, she realized that she was trapped. Quite literally. He'd cuffed her to the bed.

His plan, he'd told her, was to marry her — well, any dealer — and have them stack the tables in his favor. When she'd told him she couldn't and wouldn't do that, he'd slapped her, and did so repeatedly over the next several days. When she finally was able to get away from him, he'd tracked her down and told her again what she needed to do for him, and when she'd refused this time, he ended up sending her to the emergency room. Coleen spent the next four weeks hiding and being hurt. It wasn't until she was able to get to the stationhouse and press charges that she was able to get the divorce started. It had taken her another year and a half to get him to sign the papers. Then seven months later he was dead.

She had figured out at some point he was a little off. He'd had lists of things that he wanted her to do for him. One of them was to rob a bank, and another had been for her to run in the Miss Universe pageant. It took her an hour to make him understand that by marrying her, he'd fucked that up. She was no longer single. Micky wasn't a bad man, just not very smart. That's why this entire thing with the bills had surprised her.

Turning up the radio to drown out her thoughts, she tried to think at what point she'd become such an idiot. Coleen had gone to college, graduated with honors with a culinary degree, and had been on her way to making a name for herself. She only worked part time at the casino to make some extra money to buy her first home. Then after she'd gotten that, she'd wanted a newer car. That had never happened, along with a lot of other plans that she'd had. All because she'd been the *fancy*, as he'd called her, to a man that had no idea what he was up to most of the time. And now he'd ruined her from the grave without giving her any idea why he'd done it.

Coleen wasn't sure if she'd really been his fancy or someone that had been in the wrong place at the wrong time. But it was the only reason she could come up with for him marrying her. She oftentimes wondered if he'd drugged her too. Not even the chapel that she'd supposedly gone to could believe it when she'd been brought in. The man who ran the place, an Elvis impersonator, had told her she had seemed intoxicated and not really into her new husband. There were no recordings of the nuptials, and the marriage had been filed correctly. Coleen wondered, not for the first time, if things would ever go her way.

"I'll never trust another man, that's for sure." She looked at the radio when it just popped twice and went out. "See? Can't even trust a fucking car."

Coleen drove until she was simply too tired to go on. Pulling into a rest area, she made her way to the bathroom with her things and cleaned up. It was the best she could do, she knew that; but she still would love to have had a nice deep tub with a million bubbles. After brushing her teeth, she made her way back to her car to sleep for a few hours. At the rate she was going, she was going to need to be hosed off outside when she got to Ohio before her grandma would allow her into the house.

As soon as she closed her eyes, the tears started. They were useless, she knew that. As much as she hated to shed them, there was just no stopping them these days. She wasn't depressed, just really sad. How had things come to this? It was a question that she had no answer for. Coleen wasn't even sure there was one.

For the next fifteen years, more if she didn't get a job soon, the law firm would be taking more than half of what she made. It didn't matter if there were tips involved; she'd have to declare a percentage of whatever the check would be even if she didn't make that much in tips to cover it. Micky had put her in debt for over a hundred and fifty-three thousand dollars. Lucky for her, or them, they only wanted to collect half. Like she had seventy-six thousand dollars just laying around.

"And let's not forget the funeral costs. The fucking bastard even stuck me for that." Why he'd needed the best of everything was beyond her, but Harry had shown her what the bill had come to, as well as a prearrangement form that he'd filled out at some point. That was another thing that surprised her. Micky had seemed to live in the now, not ever thinking of the future.

Who was going to give a shit if he was in an oak casket with silk trim when he was in the dirt? That was another twenty-three thousand dollars, because he'd decided that instead of just calling hours like a normal person would have, he wanted a wake, with steak and lobster served to his mourners. Had Coleen had any idea she would have put a stop to it. But at the time she thought she wasn't his wife and was not responsible for his bill.

Selling her home and cashing in all her money had only paid a few bills. The rest, every charge card that he'd forged her name to, every charge that he'd put to every store along the strip, was now something that she'd be paying forever, it

10

would seem. All because she was pretty, he'd said.

As the sun was coming up on yet another fucked up day, she gathered her things and went to the bathroom to clean up again. Coleen got a soda from the vending machine, and looked longingly at the overpriced candy bars there. Turning her back on them, she went to her car and started out again. Her plan was to eat only at lunch, and then at a buffet. It was cheating, she knew, taking carry out from those kinds of restaurants, but it might be the only way she could eat decently for the next week.

It was going to be a very long week too. And she'd be on the road for Christmas, which was only a few days away. Crying again as she started out, she realized that she needed to get a grip on herself. She wasn't a whiny person, had never been one to let people walk all over her, but she was as stressed as she'd ever been, and felt like the weight of the world was around her neck. Coleen just wanted one or two things to go her way. She thought even that was too much to ask though.

~~~

"Christmas is in three days. Are you ready for it?" Tony wasn't sure how he was supposed to be ready when all he had to do was show up with some gifts and be cheerful, but he nodded at Micah. "Did you even decorate your house?"

"I just moved in about an hour ago, so no, I've not decorated. And since it's just me living there, I don't really care to go to the trouble of putting up a tree by myself and then having the job of taking it down again." Micah nodded and Tony realized he was distracted. "Did you get the elephant that I sent you? I also managed to snag a snake or two. They should arrive by courier sometime on Christmas morning. I think Reggie will love it, don't you?"

"Yes, yes. What did you get for Grandma and Grandda? Did you get the luggage set that I told you about?" Tony thought this was just too much fun. He told him he'd gotten them four sets. And that he'd made sure they were the ugliest colors that the store had had. "And did you wrap them or have them wrapped? I want this to be perfect."

"It's going to fail. All of it is going down the tubes with you right at the end of it. They're going to be calling the holiday fucked up day rather than Christmas after this, all because you failed." Micah looked at him as if he'd just found out he was there. "Are you back now? If you're going to berate me about something, the least you can do is pay attention to me."

"It's the girls' first Christmas, and we just heard that the little boy that we were going to take for the holidays might come to us permanently. His parents just don't want him." Tony told him congratulations, but he still wasn't sure that Micah was paying attention to him. "How can someone just say, 'I don't want a part of my body' like that? I mean, it's their child. Created by them with passion. I just don't understand how anyone can do that. She was leaving the hospital and said she wasn't going to take him at all."

"The child will be better off with you guys anyway...you know that as well as I do. And he'll be loved, not just by you, but all of us." Micah nodded. "What's really eating at you? You're acting like a man who is going to the gallows, not getting ready for the best time of the year."

Micah didn't look as if he was going to answer, but Tony

could wait him out. Something was bothering him, and until he got some help with it, he was going to stew himself into being sick. Tony had been doing that a lot himself lately…worrying about shit he had no control over.

"Before I forget to tell you, Bethany and Amanda said to tell you that they're going to join us for Christmas Eve dinner. That was really great of Reggie to invite them." Micah nodded and said he liked them both. "Did you get her anything? Amanda, I mean?"

"I did. I'm sure all of us did. She's come right into our hearts like she belonged there. Her dad is going to get to come back early too. Hardship discharge. Reggie is swinging it for him. And he's going to be honorably discharged too. Don't tell them, it's a surprise to all three." Tony knew that it was hard on the elderly woman raising a little girl. He'd been talking to Bethany a lot lately. The woman was really worried about her granddaughter too, the one coming home soon. "Did you get the cell phone delivered to Coleen, her granddaughter, like you said you were going to?"

"Yes. We have no idea where she might be, but I had one sent to each of the bigger cities along the route she told Bethany she was taking. They'll use them for something if they don't find her, but they're watching for her. I have a friend that is supposed to give her some cash, and I've reimbursed him for taking it to all the places where the phones are. I don't know if the police will find her, but hopefully she'll hook up with them and not break down on some secondary road. I can't imagine going on a trip that far without some sort of way to contact people." Micah said had he known, they could have sent the plane for her. "Yeah, I thought of that too. Hopefully she'll be able to contact Bethany soon and she'll feel better. Now tell me what has you all twisted up. It's not just this little boy either."

Bethany had shared with him how broke her granddaughter was. And why. Her ex-husband had done a number on her. She'd had to sell her home and everything of value that she'd owned, and it still hadn't been enough. Even the cell phone had cost much more than Coleen could handle at the moment. But when she arrived, if she did, there was not just a place for her to live, but a job too if she wanted it. The news that she had some cooking experience had made Elroy Baker jump right on hiring her, sight unseen. He just hoped the man wasn't taking on more than he could handle with this girl. Tony didn't much care for the new chef, and thought him a lush.

"I've been worried over Mom." Tony asked him what had been going on with Mom. "She's doing too much. I think she might be spreading herself too thin, and I'm worried that she'll get sick."

"I think she's happy working at Faerie Tales and Dreams, don't you?" Micah said she was but that was not what he meant. "Then I don't understand why you'd think she's overworking herself."

"She also works at the shelter, at the school, as well as helping us out with the girls when she's here. Did you know that she and Grandma had a fight the other day?" Tony said that he'd been unpacking and not heard. "Grandma wanted Mom to slow down and to take it easy. I guess they were working on the Christmas thing for the pack when Mom just keeled over. Grandma said it scared her to death. Mom insisted she was fine, but Grandma was too worried to let it go and made a big deal out of it, and Mom blew up at her. I asked Mom about it and she got angry with me too."

"You have Chris or one of the others look?" Micah shook his head. "I'd be talking to someone who can have a look without Mom knowing. I know that it's underhanded, but it worries me too that she fell over. Was she hurt or anything?"

"No, she just said she was tired and got a little dizzy. I know that we're all immortal, but that doesn't lessen the fact that she's our mom and not well." Tony agreed. "I was wondering, since you're almost the baby and all, if you'd go and talk to her. She likes you a great deal more than she does me right now."

"Oh, so you want me thrown under the Mom bus. I see how you are." Micah said he was worried. "I am too, but what if she takes all my gifts back? I saw my name on a lot of those packages under that tree. I'd love to be strong enough to open them."

"I'll make sure you get them." They both laughed. "So you'll do it? You'll talk to her and find out what's going on for us?"

"Yes, I will…but you owe me." Micah told him anything. "You might not think that's such a good idea when I figure out what it might be."

"To know that Mom is only tired and not sick, I'll do it. Even dance naked in the streets if that is what you want." Tony thought that had some merit to it, but only smiled. "Christ, you have no idea how much better this has made me feel already."

"She might just tell me to fuck off too." Micah said he didn't think she would. "Why? Because you think she has some sort of different love for me? I'm pretty sure that she loves us all equally."

"She does, but you're her baby boy. Well, second baby boy. She has special feelings for you on that score." Tony told him he was full of shit. "That too."

When he left for his new home, he thought about his mom. She was the best, always there for them, and kept them straight. Any of them could go to her for anything and she'd tell them not what they wanted to hear, but what they needed to hear about whatever problem they had. Tony decided to go and see her, just to see if she was really doing all right. He pulled up in front of Faeries Tales and Dreams, where he knew she'd be; or would be soon enough.

The nursery/greenhouse was busy. He'd known it would be even before it had opened. Being the week before Christmas and a new place in town, people were coming in to see what sort of things they might be able to get at the last minute. His mom was at the cash register ringing out a woman who had two carts full of things. He kissed his mom on the cheek and started to wrap the pretty little ornaments in the tissue paper on the counter.

"Maybeth, you remember my boy, Tony. Tony, this is Sarah's mom. She just came in to see if we had any more of the furniture for the gardens." Tony thought it looked like she might have cleaned them out, she had so many of them. "I was just telling her about the summer items we have coming in. You going to put any pots on your porch?"

"I don't know right now." He started to tell her just what he'd told Micah, he'd just moved in, but he looked at her face.

She was making a sale and he was fucking it up for her. "Yes. I want to get them, but I'm not sure how many right now. I've got a big wrap around porch that I think can hold about two dozen; don't you think, Mom?"

"Oh yes, and around your back deck too." He nodded, not sure what went on a back deck that didn't go on the front, but she smiled at him. "You should see his home, Maybeth. It's a beautiful sight to behold. I'm hoping that he'll have some decorations up for next Christmas; we have so many here to choose from."

He looked around. The place looked like a grocery store when a big storm was going to hit. The shelves were a little bare; the trees that had been decorated were devoid of much more than a few items. The shelves for the faerie items, a huge hit for the nursery, were mostly empty as well; even the displays had been picked clean. He looked again at the cart that his mom had yet to empty. The woman had spent a great deal of money here, and his mom had been responsible for that, he knew it. After Maybeth left with a promise of being called when the new shipments came in, he hugged his mom.

"You came here just to give me a hug?" He told her of course. "Yes, well, pull the other leg. I'm not buying it. Which one sent you, Micah or Reggie? Or was it your grandma? I'm sort of upset with her too." He sat on the counter and smiled at her. "Spill it, young man, I'm too busy to mess with you."

"You have no idea what my house looks like, because every time I want you to come out, you're off on some project. And when I invited you to lunch yesterday, you didn't show." She told him she'd forgotten, but had been busy. "Yes, I'm beginning to see that you're really busy. With other people."

"Don't try that guilt on me. I have a life too. Or I'm trying to make one. So what if I fell over? It's not that big of a deal. I'm sure you have as well at some point lately." He told her that he'd not fallen since he was a baby, and she knew it. "I'm just trying to be helpful to Pip and her new venture."

"Micah wanted me to come and see what's up. I think he thought I'd come here, talk to you a bit, and you'd just tell me. You won't, so I'm not even going to try that way. But I am going to find out what's going on. And you are not trying to help Pip. You're avoiding things, and I want to know why." He could see her temper rising, but he didn't let it get to him. She was his mom and like the rest, he was worried about her. "Mom, that's not going to work with me and you know it. You can bluster and be pissy all you want, but I'm going to know why you're avoiding us and getting sicker by the day for overworking yourself."

"Micah and Joey have their families all set. Nolan and Rylee get along so well that I'm not sure that they even finish a sentence when they're together. Burke loves his new job and his mate, as it should be. He takes such good care that she's happy and not depressed all the time, and I love him all the more for it. Garth is out making money hand over fist. You have a new home that is all complete and not in need of a mother's touch. Even your grandparents have their own things going on. Howie has his own business ventures. Since the nursery opened Katie has been in more flower clubs than I knew existed. And here I stand, all by myself, feeling like I've missed the boat somewhere along the line." He told her he loved her very much. "And I love all of you, but I miss your father."

That surprised him. His dad had been gone almost twenty-two years, and she was now missing him? Tony knew there was more, a lot more, but he stood up and hugged her.

"My home needs you very much. I have the things I want in it, but it feels cold and lonely. It's why I wanted you to come out. I have boxes everywhere, but I don't want to unpack. I feel lonely too." He lifted his mom's chin up and looked at her. "Why are you missing Dad so much right now, Mom?"

"He would be so happy with all that you boys are doing. He'd be helping with decorations in the yard like he used to do. There would be menus going around, things that you boys like the most, and how we were going to incorporate them into the meal. The grandchildren would be spoiled with gifts; not that I haven't done that, but I find myself thinking of him with each purchase and it saddens me." Tony felt his own sadness take him a little. "I'm trying to keep busy so that it doesn't hurt so much that I feel like a fifth wheel right now."

"Oh, Mom, you are anything but a fifth wheel. You hold us together; you always have. Dad would be so proud of you." She wiped at his tears and hers. "Mom, I love you so much. I don't know what I'd do without you in my life. And that being said, I need for you to take a break, come to my house, and show me how to put a lap blanket on the back of my couch so that it looks homey, not staged. How to put my canisters on the counter so that they don't look like I stood across the room and tossed them there. And for the love of all that is holy, can you please tell me what I'm supposed to do with five bedrooms, and a living room that looks like I could host a thousand people

19

in it?"

"Oh, my dear boy, you are the very best." He told her that he knew that. "I'm sorry. I guess I should tell everyone else that I'm sorry too."

"Nah, let them stew around about it for a while. But I really think you should take it easy. Not quit working, because I know how much fun you're having, but come back to us. We need you too." She nodded. "And since I know there is someone here that can take over for you, why don't you come out to my house, have some dinner, and help me out? I hate the way my house feels so cold."

"You just need a woman's touch." He nodded. "I'm sorry, baby. I truly am. But I'll help you out. No telling when you might find the right girl."

He had to tell her, soon he knew, that his own mate had died. As she went back to find someone to take over for her, he looked around again and had to smile. The trees were already redecorated and the shelves looked as full as they'd been on opening day. Magic could really make a place look good, he thought. He wondered what it would look like when spring rolled around. Christ, this place would be beautiful.

Anthony

CHAPTER 2

Coleen was exhausted. And starving. Her money was really running low and she wasn't going to make it, not at this rate. She thought about finding herself a part-time job, just for a week to get some cash, but she really wanted to get to her grandma. Everything would be all right once she was there. It wouldn't be, of course, but she had that in her head and it kept her going.

"Not fucking likely. Nothing is ever going to be all right." She was also sick of crying. All she ever seemed to do anymore was bawl about something that was a done deal. "I'm such a loser."

Just as she was reaching for the heat again to see if she could get it to at least keep her feet from burning, she saw the lights behind her. The blue and red flashing meant she'd done something wrong yet again. Pulling over, Coleen awaited her fate. Perhaps, she thought, they'd take her to jail and she'd have food and warmth.

The officer touched his knuckles to her window and she

rolled it down. "Ms. Greer?" Her blood seemed to stop moving in her body. How the fuck did he figure her name out? "Could you show me your driver's license, please? I don't want to alarm you, but I have something for you. If you could wait—"

"Is it my grandma? Is she hurt? Oh God, please, don't let anything happen to her. She's a wonderful person and I love her to death." He assured her that no one was hurt. "Then how did you know it was me?"

"The entire state has been looking for you. If you'd just...." He asked her to wait while he went back to his car.

The entire state had been watching for her to pull her over? That didn't seem right. What the fuck had she done now? As she sat there, a million and a half things ran through her mind. She'd paid her personal bills, what little there had been. Tipped well, even though she could have used the money when she'd no longer been able to go without some food. And she'd made sure that she paid for each place she'd had to stop for gas. When he came back to the car, Coleen was sobbing.

"I'm so sorry. I don't know what I did, but please don't take me to jail. I thought I wanted to go...I'm hungry and cold, you see. The heater doesn't work unless it's to blast me with hot or cold air; there is no in-between for it. Nor does the radio so I can drown out my sorrow by turning it up. I've been feeling sorry for myself for a long time—well, since Micky fucked up my life—but...." She looked up at the officer. "I'm so sorry. I'm stressed out."

"I'd say that was an understatement. Here, you take this and I'll have a look under your hood to see why the heater might not be working. Just turn off your car please." She did as he asked and took the box and thick envelope. "Remember, I'm under the hood, so don't blow your horn or take off. I don't want to be hurt."

The box she opened first. It wasn't huge, but it was heavy. As soon as she tore the paper off it, she could see that it was a cell phone. And it was a really nice one. Turning it on, she read the note that was in the box with it.

"It's charged so you can use it right away. I had your grandma's number put in it so you could call her immediately. She's very worried about you." There was no signature on the bottom and she'd looked for one twice. Unlocking the phone, she saw the only number on it was her grandma, and there was a picture of who she could only assume was her niece. Putting the phone down for now, she picked up the envelope.

The cash fell out on her lap. Shaking, she picked it up one bill at a time and counted it. There was two thousand dollars in the envelope, and no note. Getting out of her car with the phone and the money, she went to find the officer.

"You need a new radiator cap." She nodded. "If you just go into the next town, I can show you a place to get one. I'm off duty as of an hour ago, and—"

"Where did this come from? There is money here, as well as a fully charged phone. You said someone said to give it to me, but there isn't any indication who it was. No name. Who would do that?" He said he didn't know, but he'd been looking for her for two days. "That's another thing. How did you know to look for me? I don't have any signage on my car. I didn't do anything wrong, and I certainly didn't tell anyone but my grandma which route I was going. Who did this?"

"Three days ago volunteers were asked to work a special duty for a friend of the captain's. We were to patrol the highway for four hours at a time looking for you. It was easy to figure out what you were driving...the DMV in your town gave us the information. The man that called in the favor sent a picture of you and that stuff." He leaned against the car. "This route is the safest way to go from Vegas to Ohio, where we knew you were headed. And since we knew when you left home, it was pretty easy to estimate when you'd be getting here. But I'm to understand there are four other envelopes with a box along this same route in the event someone missed you."

"I don't understand this. Why would anyone care which way I came and that I didn't have a phone?" He said he didn't know. "Maybe my grandma knows something."

"Could be." The officer stood up. "I will tell you that it's been a real pleasure looking for you. Trying to figure out why you'd have someone going to a lot of trouble and expense to get you that stuff. I take it there is something there that will help you along?"

"I'm broke. I've not had a good meal in...well, forever it seems. I'm going on fumes, and wasn't sure I was going to make it another day." He grinned at her. "What do you get out of this? This person on the other end...did he promise you something that I might give you? I'm not going to, if that's what you're hoping."

"No ma'am. And I can understand why you're distrusting. I looked you up." She nodded, feeling stupid for what she'd said to him. "If you'll just follow me into town, I'll show you the place to get a cap and good meal. Might not be the best, but

24

it's rib sticking, and Benny can make a good breakfast if you're into carb loading."

"Right now, so long as it's not a candy bar or a granola bar, I'm for it." She went back to her car and started it. Waiting for him to pull out in front of her, she put the phone away. She wouldn't drive and talk on the phone, but she was itching to call her grandma. Not just to find out what was going on, but to just talk to her. It had been too long.

After he got a cap for her radiator and replaced her old one with it, he showed her where to go for food. Coleen turned to him. He was looking at her like he knew a great secret, but she was too tired and hungry to try and figure it out.

"I'm sorry for what I implied back there. I've have a rough month or so." He nodded and told her he understood. "I don't usually bite the hand that feeds me, and I was way out of line with you. Whoever this other person is, I owe him more than I can ever repay. I'm really down on my luck here."

"I talked to a buddy of mine in Vegas. He thinks you were hosed. Said you should find a good attorney and go back and get this straightened out. Thinks it isn't your fault that no one checked to make sure whether you were divorced or not." She told him she was too broke to hire anyone else. "Well, then, I'm sorry to hear that. Truly I am. But you have a nice dinner, get a hotel, and call your grandma. She's been worried over you."

"And I her."

After he left, she made her way to the diner he'd recommended. So long as it was hot and didn't come from a vending machine, she was ready for it. As soon as she walked in, she knew that she was going to love it. Picking up the phone after ordering, she called her grandma.

"Oh child, I've been worried sick over you." Coleen felt her tears fall again and didn't care who saw her. "When Tony suggested this idea of his, I nearly wept with joy, I tell you. You weren't scared, were you? I wondered if them pulling you over would scare you a little."

"The officer was wonderful. And he fixed my car for me. The heat wasn't working. We don't have a lot of use for heat out where I live...lived." She thought of her home and her things. "I'm going to spend the night here in this town and then head out in the morning. I want to take a long hot bath, then sleep in a bed. The car wasn't made for resting in. And the money, you have no idea how handy that's going to be."

"Money? Well, I suppose he'd think of that too. Such a lovely man. He got his mom and sisters to get little Mandy some things to wear when she got here. Carol didn't even get her a proper pair of boots." Alarms were going on in her head. Some man was buying things for her niece? And he'd sent her money without her grandma knowing? He was up to something, no doubt. Well, he was in for it when she got there. "Are you there, sweetheart?"

"Yes. I was just thinking about this man. What do you know about him? I mean, why would he do this for me when I have no idea who he is?" She told him. "So this family, they're taking you under their wing because they're rich and have too much money."

"I didn't say that. I said they were nice and that they have money." Coleen knew that her grandma was upset with her, but Coleen knew people better than she did. "He and his family help out a lot of people when they need it. Mostly veterans, but they help all the townspeople. And Mandy just loves Tony to death."

"I bet." Her mind was going in all sorts of directions on that as well. "I should be home in three days. I'm sorry about Christmas, but we'll have a lot more time to be together from now on. And Sheppard will be home soon too."

"All right, but I'd like for you not to judge these people before you meet them, Coleen. They really are a nice bunch of people, and them buying things for your niece was something that helped me as well." Coleen told her she'd try. "You call me when you want, all right? I'd love to hear from you now and again."

"I will call you when I take a break. And let that man know that I'll pay him back somehow for doing this for you. It's going to be helpful, but I won't be beholden to anyone again." Her grandma just said she'd talk to her later. "I love you."

When the line went dead after Grandma told her she loved her as well, Coleen felt horrible. She'd hurt the only person in the world besides her brother who meant anything to her. As soon as she got there she was going to make it up to her. Somehow.

~~~

Tony was pulling the last box of gifts from his car when he saw Bethany coming up the driveway. It was going to be a lovely Christmas Eve here at home, and he was really glad that the two of them could join his family. He knew that Bethany's granddaughter had gotten the phone, and hoped that she'd called her grandma by now. Mandy came running to him almost as soon as their car stopped.

"Hello, sweat pea. How are you this fine cold day?"

She told him about her tree and the candy canes that she'd eaten, and about everything else she'd done since he'd seen her yesterday. Bethany was walking toward him with several gift bags in each hand, and he went to help her.

"Oh my, she's having a good time. And after hearing from Coleen, I'm feeling more in the spirit myself." Tony helped her to the porch before setting down her bags. "Your family was mighty nice for asking the two of us over when it's a family thing. I thought about not coming, but Mandy wouldn't hear of it."

"I would have come to get you had you not shown up. And we open our home to a lot of people on Christmas. You'll see that when you go in." Bethany nodded, but he could tell she had something on her mind. "Mandy, can you take these things in to Micah for me? He'll know just where they go."

After she was gone, he looked at the elderly woman. She was visibly upset, and he wondered what he or someone else might have done to her. When he went back to his car to get his own packages, she stood there waiting.

"Coleen has been hurt really bad, I told you that." Tony nodded. "She's not too trusting. Never has been really; always looking for someone to take something back when they gave it to her. Probably because of her mom, Carol, and Micky, but I don't know. Sheppard used to be as bad, but I think the service changed him some."

"She doesn't like that I sent her money and a phone." Bethany nodded. "I should have told you about the money.

28

But after calling in a few favors and Grandda doing the same, I found out that she was dead broke. And figured she could use a little help."

"Coleen said she was going to pay you back. I know that you were helping us, but she's not trusting, as I said." She looked at the house then back at him. "I told her you were helping me out with little Mandy. So I got to thinking about some of the things she said, and I think she has it in her head you're a pervert. I don't know why she'd think that but for me telling her how Mandy loves you and all."

"I see. You know that I'd never harm you or Mandy, don't you?" Bethany said she knew that. "Was Coleen hurt as a child, Bethany?"

It was difficult for her to answer; he could see that. And he might not have asked, but she was going to be living in their town and they would see each other. He didn't want to have to worry each time he saw this woman that she was going to cause him trouble.

"I don't know, to be honest with you. Her mom—my daughter—was...she wasn't very smart about a lot of things. And having those two babies as young as she did, I think she lost out on a lot of growing up, so she felt like she had to make up for it after they were here. She was just sixteen when she had them. I tried my best to help her out, but she was high strung and thought that her way was best. Like most teenagers, I guess. I think those two suffered by her hand more than they should have." Tony asked her where the mom was now. "She was killed. Robbery, they say, but I think that sooner or later something else would have taken her. The kids went their own way a long time before that, both of them leaving their mom at the same age she gave them life. I know for a little bit they stayed with Carol, but that didn't last long. I didn't hear a thing from either of them for about a few years after their mom had passed."

"I'm sorry about that. And if she insists on paying me back, I'll take it. I only wanted her to make it here safely, for you." Bethany nodded. "What else? There is something more, isn't there?"

"Yes. I'm not sure.... You're not human, are you, Tony? I'm assuming that your family isn't. I mean, I heard rumors and all, but...are you?" He shook his head. "I see. You may want to know why I asked, but to be honest with you, I don't have a reason, other than I just wanted to know the truth of it. I won't tell anyone. I promise you that."

"I know that, Bethany. And I'm glad that you asked." She nodded and picked up the two bags that Mandy hadn't come back for. "I won't ever harm you. None of us will. But I must warn you that not all the occupants of the house today are human either. Very few of them are, as a matter of fact."

"Will they be okay with us here?" He told her they were thrilled to meet them. "And my granddaughter, do you suppose she'll be thrilled as well? She's not cruel, but she is a little on the cautious side when it comes to people, men especially. I'd like for you and yours to give her some time."

"We'll give her whatever she needs. Even if she doesn't want it." Bethany nodded and laughed when he did. "Now, let's go and get some food and gifts. I, for one, can't wait to see Mandy's face when she sees the gifts we got her."

"You'll spoil her." He told her he hoped so. "Such a lovely man. Where were you when my granddaughter was single?"

"Hiding." She grinned at him as they entered the house. "I think the two of us wouldn't have set well. She sounds like a woman who likes things her own way. And I am a man who likes the same thing. I'm young, but set in my ways deeper than my Grandda is."

"You act like him too."

After they made their way into the living room with their arms loaded, Garth went out with him to bring in the rest. He was still thinking about the compliment that Bethany had given him, and nearly fell on his ass when Garth told him that he'd gotten his commission off the deal that he'd made for him.

"You seriously sold it for more than I was asking? Damn, but that's wonderful news." Garth told him that he could invest it for him, all fourteen million dollars if he wanted. "Yes, please do. I just want to get a few things with it first. A bigger truck, and I'd really like to buy the grade school downtown that's for sale. The one that I was telling you about."

"Yeah, the one you want to turn into an office for you. Got news for you big brother, you own it too. And the one to the left of it. I was able to swing a deal with that too when I purchased the two apartment buildings just behind it. I knew that you wanted it, and had the city throw them in at the last minute. To be honest, I think they were thrilled to get them off the books. And with the new businesses going in, it'll be worth more in a few years rather than less." Tony hugged his brother. "Man, this has been one hell of a year. I'm almost afraid to see what the next one brings."

"I know just what you mean. Christ, I would like for one month to go by when we have a good time and nothing happens to anyone." They loaded each other up and headed to the house. "I got Mom something extra for helping me out the other day. My house already looks homier."

"You should see what she did at my house last week. I invited her over for dinner and she helped me move my living room around. It looks so much better. Nothing new, but it looks like it. She said I had no flow. I guess she was right; I have been spending more time in there since she left." Tony told him that she was the best. "You know it. And we're damned lucky to have her."

"Lucky to have who?" They both kissed their mom on the cheek when she met them in the hall. "No more cursing, Garth. I'd hate to have to stand you in the corner on Christmas Eve. So who is it that you're lucky to have? A mate, Garth? That would be lovely."

"No, you. We're very lucky to have you in our lives. All the family, but you especially." She hugged them both, then hugged them again. Tony loved his mom; he wasn't ashamed to admit it either.

Entering the living room where the tree was, Tony just stared at it. Christ, it looked like it was twelve feet tall and every branch had something on it. The tree practically glistened with happiness and warmth. He looked at the topper and felt tears fill his eyes. His dad's cap had been on the top of their trees since they were children. And the tradition hadn't stopped when he passed away. His dad would be so proud right now.

"All right everyone, I want you each to tell us what you're

happy for this year, along with your name. We have a great many new friends joining us this year." His mom leaned against him. "We have so much to be thankful for as well. So I'll start. My name is Gracie Bentley, and I'm happy to have all of you here with me. My husband, the love of my life, would have loved seeing this room filled with all of you. And as much as I miss him every minute of every day, I'm so very happy to have his children here to fill some of the void he left."

Tony kissed his mom on the forehead. "My name is Tony Bentley, and I'm happy that I'm not going to be the one that has to clean up this mess when we're done." His mom smacked him on the chest. "But I'm especially thankful and happy that I have the best friends and family a man could hope for. And the best role models as well."

As they made their way around the room, each of them telling a joke then something they were happy for, Tony thought that perhaps a man could ask for nothing more than what he had right in front of him. He was successful, in great shape, and had money to burn should he want to. He wouldn't, of course, but he had everything he could ever hope to need. Tony was content.

CHAPTER 3

It was close to midnight when she pulled into town. Coleen was sore and tired, but she was home. Now all she had to do was remember where her grandma lived. It had been a long time since she'd been here, and things had changed a little since then. She stopped at the light and looked again at the instructions that she'd gotten last night on the phone. Turn onto Tenth. That was all she'd written down.

"Fuck." When the light turned in her favor, she made her way through it carefully. She was trying her best not to run into anything while she read the street signs. It wasn't until she was nearly on top of it that she saw the balloons with her name on them. Smiling, she turned at the corner. There was no right, just a left. Coleen followed the balloons at every corner she needed to turn at until she got to the house. Her grandma's house looked just like she remembered, even the same God awful ugly concrete duck out front. And the entire length of the driveway was covered in balloons.

Grandma came out of the house as soon as she turned off

the engine. Coleen got out of the car and ran to her, hugging the woman who had always been there for her and her brother, even when they had pushed her away. And now here she was again, putting out her hand to pull one of them up. Coleen hugged her tightly, knowing that she had finally come home.

"Do you need anything from the car tonight?" She said that she needed her clothing. "Well, hurry on and get it and we'll get you warmed up. Boy, it sure did turn a little nippy in a short bit. They're saying it might get cold tomorrow."

Coleen thought it was fucking freezing, but she'd come from a warmer place. As she pulled her luggage free, she grabbed her purse and the rest of her things from the car. Locking it up, she went into the house and felt the warmth hit her like a blast from a furnace.

It wasn't just the heat, which was welcoming, but the feeling of home. She knew that her grandma didn't have much, but the things that she did have she cared for. Even the table, which her and Sheppard had eaten at the few times they'd been here, was in as good a shape as it had been all those years ago. And the curtains, ducks in a row, were worn but clean.

"You're set up in the back bedroom. Got it all warmed up for you, and linens set out for you to use if you wanna shower tonight." Coleen said that she did. "Well, I got you a surprise. Dern near had myself a heart attack, but I'm sure you're going to be loving it as much as me."

When she disappeared down the hall, Coleen set the kettle on the stove for tea. She loved her Grandma's tea, and when she heard her return she started to ask her where it was when she saw the man standing there.

"Sheppard? Oh my God, Sheppard!" She ran to him and wrapped herself around him. Christ, it had been ten years since she'd seen him, and he looked wonderful. "When did you get in? When do you have to go back? Oh God, I can't believe you're here too. I've missed you so much."

"I'm home, for good. I apparently have friends in some very high places, and they pulled some strings and got me out a little earlier. I've been here a few days to surprise Mandy for Christmas." She hugged him again, holding him to her a little longer each time. "I've missed you so much, Coleen. But you look like crap, and smell."

She hit him and told him she'd been driving for two days straight. "I wanted to make it by Christmas, but I got stuck in a storm on the interstate and couldn't make it. Oh, but you're here. It's wonderful that we're all here." He kissed her cheek and they both hugged Grandma. "You did this? Brought him home early?"

"Oh no, I had no idea. The Bentleys, they did it. Wanted to give me something special for the holidays." The Bentleys again. Coleen wondered if they were ever going to butt out of their lives. But they had brought her brother home, and she supposed she could forgive them. "Now, we'll need to keep it down a bit. Mandy is asleep, and I want her to stay that way for now. You two can catch up in the morning. Both of you to bed."

Coleen wanted to stay up all night just to see her brother, but she was tired and she also knew that she did smell. Going into the back bedroom, she did a little dance. Her brother was home for good, and she was here where she could try and start over. Things might be looking up after all. As she entered the bathroom that she didn't think was there before, she found an envelope on the counter. Picking it up, she read it while she laid out her things.

"Job interview at ten-thirty on the twenty-ninth. The man's name is Elroy Baker, and he's opening a restaurant in the downtown area. Please bring resume." She read it three times before she set it back on the counter. Who would be setting her up for an interview in a restaurant? She decided that she'd talk to Grandma in the morning.

After taking a long hot shower and washing her hair twice, she pulled on her jammies and crawled into bed. But sleep, even as tired as she was, didn't come to her easily. Her mind, even being here, was still stuck on what had happened to her. She was, as far as she could understand, ruined. There would not be anything good coming her way for a very long time.

Rolling to her back, she thought of the Bentleys. Every time she talked to Grandma she would tell her what they'd done, who they'd helped, and how much she was beginning to depend on them. It frightened Coleen to think that someone might be scamming her grandma. No one was as nice as these people were making themselves look. She wondered then if they had anything to do with her interview.

As much as she wanted to not go to it, just because they had more than likely set it up for her, she needed a job. And money. Even with the staggering amount that was going to be taken out of her check each payday, she had to live. And since Sheppard was living here too, it was going to be a strain on Grandma to help them all out.

Rolling to her side again, she thought of Micky and his

fucked up life. The man had hurt her; not just physically, but in every other way possible too, and she had never even liked him. Crying again, wishing for just one thing to go right in her life, she had a feeling that wasn't in the cards for her. But she was so happy that Sheppard was here. He would understand why they needed to push the Bentleys away. He would help her convince their grandma.

As exhaustion rolled over her, Coleen decided that she'd find a place to move to, close enough to her grandma to help her out with Mandy, but also cheap. She wondered as she yawned if there were any furnished places in town. Because as it was right now, she didn't have a pot to pee in.

~~~

Howie saw the young woman when he was walking toward Faerie Talcs and Dreams. He had an idea that he was in trouble at home, and wanted to get a dozen or so roses for Katie before she started on him. He knew now it might have been a bad idea to get up in the middle of the night to finish off the pie in the fridge. But it had been delicious, and he'd been about to pop when he'd gone back to bed. Detouring a bit, he went into the diner and sat across from who he thought might be Bethany's granddaughter.

"Howdy." She nodded at him, but he could see right away that she'd been crying. "Ain't nothing so bad that talking about it won't help. You tell me what it is and I'll make it right."

"Really?" Howie grinned and nodded. "Okay, I'm almost a hundred thousand in debt that I will never get out from under. I had to sell my home, my furniture, and every piece of jewelry I owned to bury a bastard that fucked me over. On top of slapping me every time he saw me because I wasn't going to go against everything that I am to cheat at cards for him. My car just died. I guess I'm lucky it didn't do that on the way here, but now I have nothing. I have no money, no job, and not one thing that belongs to me other than the clothing I brought with me. Tears are all that I have right now."

"I'm sorry to hear that, darlin. I truly am." He put out his hand. "Howie Bentley. You must be Coleen Greer. Bethany was just.... Where you going?"

"No offense to you, but I've about had all I can handle of the famous Bentleys for one lifetime." He wasn't sure that was nice, but he stood up to follow her. "My grandma told me this one guy...." She looked at him with a glare. "You set me up for an interview with a famous chef. Did you really think I'd fall for that? That some famous five-star chef is going to want me, a nobody— less than nobody—to work for him?"

Howie waited until she paid her check and went outside when she did, then told her to come with him. When she stood there, glaring at him still, Howie felt something that he'd not felt in years; anger. At this little thing.

"You need to take it down a few notches and get that large log off your shoulder. I don't like being called a liar when all I wanted to do was help out a dear friend of mine." She said nothing, but the tears were falling again. "You come with me, right now."

"I don't want to." He told her he didn't really care what she wanted right now. "So what are you going to do to me if I don't follow you into some building where you can beat and hurt me? Or are you going to tie me to the bed and have someone else beat me? Is that what this is about? You have to control me and you'll do it any way you can?"

His anger was gone just like that. He watched her struggle with demons that he was sure were gonna tear her apart soon. The poor thing was hurting more than her family knew, he'd bet his last nickel on it.

"Is he dead?" She nodded at him. "Good. Because right now I'd like nothing more than to find and kill him myself. No reason to hurt someone in the first place, but to tie someone up to beat them; well, that's just not right on a great many levels. Now, you fix up your pretty face and come with me. I have something to show you."

"I'm very sorry I was nasty to you. I'm normally not so... well, I am usually nasty, but not generally so early in the morning. And Micky didn't tie me to the bed and beat me. I meant it metaphorically. That he'd tied me up and taken everything I had." He smiled at her as they crossed the street. "My grandma is mad at me. I ticked my brother off too, and I think Mandy is upset with me as well because I didn't understand what she got me for Christmas."

"It's a faerie bench." She nodded. "You haven't been around much, but I'll show you that in a bit. The nursery, Faerie Tales and Dreams...it's my granddaughter-in-law's place." She nodded at him, but he could tell she was tender yet. "You're gonna have to trust me, child. I mean you no harm today."

"I know that. I'm just dealing with some things. Personal stuff. Not that I didn't just blast you with almost every one of them, but there's more." He nodded as they continued down the sidewalk. "I don't think I've ever been this cold before.

When does it get warm around here?"

"Might be tomorrow. Ohio weather is like that. One day it could be seventy degrees, the next below zero." She shivered and he had to laugh. "You need to get a nice coat and some gloves. I'll have...no, that won't work. You got no car. Well, you come on in here and let me do some planning."

"This is a restaurant. I don't think I can afford to go in here, much less order. It's beautiful." He thanked her. "I don't know what you think is going to happen, Mr. Bentley, but if this is a joke, I don't think it's funny."

"Not a joke, not at all. Elroy has been wanting to meet you, and today is as good as the next, don't you think?" She shook her head. "I guess he could come on out here and interview you, but I'm thinking you're gonna be warmer inside. You can go on in now."

"I don't have an appointment until day after tomorrow. I wasn't even sure that I was going to go. I mean...you're a Bentley." He told her he was. "I don't even have a resume. Grandma doesn't have a computer, and the one that my brother has is pretty old and it takes too long to boot up and all. I don't know about this."

He took her arm and led her inside. Once there, he asked someone to find Elroy, and Howie watched the young woman. She was as nervous as a cat in a room full of rockers. He had to smile at that...the woman was going to shine here. Elroy came toward him and put out his hand.

"Howie, I'm not open just yet, but I have a few things that I'd like to have you test drive for me. You're the perfect person for it." Howie loved food. He supposed it was a good thing

42

he was a panther; he'd probably weigh nearly four hundred pounds if he didn't burn calories so fast. "Oh my, didn't know you had a date. Come along then, we have food to taste."

"This is the woman I was telling you about. Coleen Greer." Elroy shook her hand, but Howie knew he was as confused as the girl was. But the longer he stood there talking to his friend, the more he knew the reason for his not remembering. The drinking. "The cook to help you out."

"Oh yes. I remember. I've been…well, it's all right. Come on back and we'll get this sticky part over. Howie tells me that you've been a chef at some very nice restaurants in Las Vegas. Lovely place out there. Too busy for me, however."

As they continued to talk, Howie went to the table that had lines of food on it. He saw one of the under chefs, Matt he thought his name was, come toward him, and expected him to tell him to get lost. The man, however, handed him a plate and fork and asked him what he wanted to try.

"Well now, we might as well start at the front. You tell me what I'm going to be tasting and I'll give you my opinion." The younger man smiled and told him the first dish was poached salmon with candied lemon rinds. "I love those lemon rinds. My wife had one of them lemon cakes at Christmas that was decorated with them. Could have made a meal off of them."

"On a cake? Oh, that's a wonderful idea." Matt made a note and nodded to the dish in front of him. "Your wife must be a wonderful cook then."

"Nah, she doesn't cook at all; but she sure can find some pretty good food on the Interweb. We had some capers in something; didn't care for those, but the food around it was good." He tasted the salmon. "Now that's pretty good. Not too fishy, if you know what I mean."

After trying all the dishes and vetoing only two of them, Coleen joined him. She didn't care for the two dishes he hadn't either, but she had a thing or two to say about the salmon.

"Next time you cook it, rinse it well first. Then take the skin off, and it'll be prettier on the plate when they're finished eating." Matt asked her why that was important after they'd eaten it. "Because the plate will be sitting in front of them for a minute or two, and you don't want them to think, 'I just ate that?' No, you want them to think it was wonderful, with no ill feelings after. Presentation is key, before as well as after they're done with a good meal."

Matt nodded and made some more notes. While the two of them talked, Howie went to find his buddy. There was a thing or two that he wanted to talk to him about anyway. One of them was drinking on the job.

"Howie, you sent me a gem in her." Howie said he knew that, and sat down across from Elroy. There was an empty liquor bottle in front of him, as well as an ashtray of cigarette butts. Howie made it a point to make sure that Elroy knew he'd seen them. "I've been having some trouble resting at night. My memories, they haunt me at times, and I just can't deal with them very well. Not alone anyway."

"There ain't nothing in that bottle gonna help you with that. And them sticks there, they'll kill you for sure." Elroy nodded, but made no more excuses. "You gonna hire her? She's got some baggage. Not anything that will affect you, but she's got some anyway."

"We all do. Even you, I bet." Howie said nothing. If he had baggage, he took care of it. He didn't let it fester and grow out of control like he thought Elroy might be doing. "Yes, I hired her. Not because you asked me to have a look at her, but she's got a good reference. I checked her out at the last place she worked before she came here."

"Heard tell they didn't want her to go. But she needed a place to live while she was recovering from her day in court." Elroy nodded. Howie had had her checked out as well. "You need anything, Elroy? Want me to do something for you?"

"No. I'm just.... Maybe this was a mistake, opening this big of a place when all I wanted was quiet. But you painted such a pretty picture for me." He laughed a little. "I'm not blaming you for this. You told me it was up to me how much I was getting into, but I wanted something to take the pain away. I think it will once we get open, but right now, I'm overwhelmed in my pain of losing her."

"You'll be fine. And if you need a break or something, I'm sure you have enough good people out there to help you take it." He nodded again. "Elroy? What is it?"

"Nothing. I'm just thinking that had I not met you all those years ago, I might have become a different man. Someone that might have failed big time. You and Katie, you gave me a chance, and I'll never forget it."

"Good." Howie stood up. "Now I want you to get yourself cleaned up and comb your hair. You're a mess. Throw out this bottle and stop smoking. Nobody, especially me, wants to find cigarette ash in their food. And while I don't throw my weight around much, you ruin this for these people here, and there will never be another reason for you to take a drink to forget memories. Do you understand me?"

"Yes, I understand you. Very well. I'm not broken, but there are times when I feel close. And I don't smoke anywhere but in here, but I'll try to quit. Mary hated it as well." He stood up too, and picked up the bottle and dropped it into the trash. "There, the beginning."

Howie left him to it a few minutes later. He had a feeling that they were gonna talk again. As he made his way back to the kitchen, he wasn't surprised to see young Matt hanging on every word that Coleen told him as she did something over the stove. A young woman, a pretty little thing, was standing on her other side just absorbing the words, Howie thought.

"See how much nicer it looks when you lower the heat? The next time you want to cure the butter, turn the heat down under it and you'll have a much fluffier sauce." As the whisk in her hand moved quickly, Howie stood back. Whatever she was making, it smelled like heaven. As soon as she poured it over the salmon that he'd had a bite of, he felt his mouth water.

"What're you making there?" Matt told him hollandaise sauce. "And you put it over the fish like that? Let me try it. I'll tell you what I think."

With his first bite he knew that he was tasting perfection. The hollandaise sauce was as smooth as butter, and just as rich as Midas. Howie moaned as he was taking a second taste.

"It's good on all sorts of meats. Pork, if you add just a little fried apple to it. Even vegetables." He nodded as Coleen put another plate next to the salmon. "Here, try this. It's my own sauce that I made at the other place. It's so good you'll want to lick the plate when you've eaten all the chicken. Or so I've been told."

The chicken was in thin slices that had been breaded and fried. He could see the crispness under the batter even before he cut into the tender slice. When Coleen encouraged him to take the sauce with it, he dipped the chicken in it and took it to his mouth. Howie felt his mouth come alive with the flavors. Then Matt and Tansy, her name tag said, tried it.

"This is amazing." Howie had to agree. "This is…wow, this is going to be a hit, I know it. What would you serve this with? I'm thinking pasta with a little butter on it."

"No, spiral cut zucchini and squash that has been browned a little in butter. Then a pinch of cumin to give it a little bite. The sauce would be served on the side so that if they wanted to pour it over all the dish, it would be their choice. Most people did and loved it. Good for dipping bread in as well." Howie reached for the bread that she was slicing and dipped a generous slice into it. "The bread would be grilled too, just to give it a little extra strength to take the sauce."

Howie was positive that they'd hired the wrong chef to run this place. And by the time he left, he was so full he was pretty sure he'd not have to eat for a week. In the two hours they were there, Coleen had made them three more dishes and even a small plate of dessert, and not once had Elroy come out of his office. Howie was worried about him, and a good deal mad. The man was going to be a problem, he was thinking.

"I owe you an apology." He asked Coleen why she thought that. "I didn't think there was a restaurant, first of all, and Baker really being there was a surprise as well. This isn't a place where I would have thought him to settle down."

"He lost his way a bit after his wife died." She said he was drunk. "Yes, he was at that. But he said he was gonna stop. Are you gonna work for him?"

"Yes. I need the money he's offering me and you know it. Also, to work with a man like him will open doors for me once, if ever, I get out from under my debt." Howie nodded. "I'm sure that you're aware of why I'm here. Just as well as you know that man in there isn't going to stop drinking. He has a taste for it now; not the liquor itself, but the numbness it gives him when he's deep into it. The only way he's going to stop is death, or if someone takes him by the collar and shoves him in a cell."

"I'm sure he thinks he will." Coleen just looked away. "You this blunt all the time? The reason I'm asking is, I think you might fit in well with my family."

"Mr. Bentley, I'm barely hanging on right now. As you've figured out, I have nothing to my name but this job now. I know who you are...Grandma can talk of nothing else but the great and powerful Bentleys, and how they swooped in and saved the poor little old woman from the great banker. Not quite the story, but the premise is the same." He laughed, liking her more all the time. "But I don't want saving; I might need it, but I don't want it. I have to do this on my own, stand up for myself. I could have used it a few years ago, but I'm not going to let anyone take over for me again. And when I can save a little money, I'm going to buy a home, small but it'll be mine, and live out the rest of my life as quietly and peacefully as I can. I don't want anyone in my life that's not related to me. People

48

suck."

"They do at that. But I have a feeling that we're gonna cross paths a lot more than you think." She asked him why. "Because I own the place you work at."

CHAPTER 4

The house was coming along. He did all the things on the list that his mom had given him, and had even gone to the local Goodwill to pick up a couple of things for the yard. Who would have thought that painting an old screen door would make such a wonderful trellis for his roses? Tony made his way into the house again, and stopped suddenly when a large man stood up from the kitchen table.

"Can I help you?" He nodded but said nothing. "I'm not sure where you're supposed to be, but this is my home and I don't want to have to call the police to—"

"Daniel James. Your momma said that you needed a cook." She had? First he'd heard of it. "I was working at the diner until last week when I lost my house."

"How does one lose a house?" He told him it was a fire that wasn't his fault. "I see. And she hired you because you lost your home? I'm sorry, but she didn't say anything to me about this."

"No sir, she said I was to come here and to tell you…remind

you about the salad. I'm not sure what that's about, but she was sure you'd know." Tony said he did and smiled. "I'm guessing you don't need me around then."

"No, I think my mother had it right." Daniel nodded and smiled. "The salad, in case you were wondering...I don't cook. Not even sure what I'm supposed to do with the equipment that's in here. I mean, I can use the microwave if I have to, but I'd rather just go out. Anyway, Mom came here for dinner, and all I had was a salad. It had been in the fridge for over a week. I'm pretty sure you can guess how nasty that was."

"Pretty bad. Did you have the dressing on it already?" Tony said that the tomatoes had looked like a science project too. "Oh my goodness. Well, she was right then, you need yourself a cook. But I have to tell you, I'm more of a butler than a cook. I can whip up something if I have a recipe, but not anything from scratch."

"But she hired you as a cook." He said he'd been hired as a go to man for him. "My mom is very strange. Did you catch that?"

"Yes, sir, I did. But I don't think I'll be saying that to her. Not to her face anyway." Tony told him he was a smart man. "Yes, when it comes to women, I think I can be."

Tony came the rest of the way in the house and put his painting things on the mudroom floor before taking his shirt off. He was nasty feeling and hungry. When he was standing in only his jeans, he looked at Daniel.

"How do we make this work? I mean, I'm not used to having someone around, and I'm assuming that since you have no home, you'll be staying here, correct?" Daniel told him he'd like to stay in the house out by the fence line. Tony was pretty sure that there hadn't been a house there when he'd moved in, but said nothing as he nodded. He wasn't even sure he'd ever seen a fence back there. This magic stuff was pretty tricky, he thought.

"I got my things. What little the firemen could save for me anyway. I guess the place is furnished too?" Tony was sure it was now and nodded again. "You don't talk much, do you?"

"No. And when you meet my grandda, you'll think that I'm a mute. He'll talk your arm off." Daniel laughed. "I have to shower and get ready to go into town for a little while. If you could make me something...I guess a light snack, I'd appreciate it. I'm supposed to have dinner at the new restaurant with my family. Would you like to go?"

"No sir, but I thank you for the invite. I have some moving in to do, and I'll make up a list of stuff I need to start out with here in the kitchen. Your mom, she said that there was magic here? That I could just put out a list and it would be filled?" Tony told him that was how it had worked for him. "All right then. You shower, and I'll get you a light snack going."

He took his time washing up. Tony decided not to ask his mom about Daniel. When she was ready to confess to him that she'd gone behind his back, he'd tell her that he liked the man. In the meantime, he'd let her think he was mad. Tony pulled out his suit and pulled on the pants.

He hated dressing up. Wearing a tie to him was the equivalent of being hanged by your own socks. So when he pulled his tie from the closet he simply put it over his shoulder rather than tie it just yet. If he got to the place and everyone had theirs off, he wasn't going to bother. As soon as he entered the kitchen, he knew that he'd made a good choice in letting the man stick around.

"Not too light, I'm afraid, but it'll stick with you well enough." A thick roast beef sandwich was laid out on a platter with a mountain of chips. "I found some tea in the fridge too if you want it. Not sure if it's sweet or not."

"It's not." When he took his first bite of the sandwich, he looked at Daniel when he was finished chewing. "You know that I'm not human, right? Mom told you?"

"Yes, sir, she did. Said that I'd have to be on the lookout for some little people that might come around. Faeries, she said." Tony told him that there were two in the house, but at the moment, he didn't know where they were. "One of them is up on the curtain. The other is still in the pantry making a list. I asked him if he needed me to write for him, and he explained that he'd just bring it in. I'm assuming that he has that sort of power."

Daniel had said it so calmly while he refilled his glass of tea that Tony laughed. Yes, they were going to get along just fine.

When he was finished, the two faeries came and sat on the table and introduced themselves to Daniel. Gom and Awnia had been here since he moved in, and they'd gotten along just fine in all that time.

By the time he left, Tony thought that his household was complete. He wasn't sure that he'd actually needed a go to man, what Daniel had said he was when he wasn't cooking, but he was glad for the company too. His mom was going to have a bit of explaining to do to, Tony thought.

Anthony

Tony stopped by his new building. He'd been by the day before, but the workers had been too numerous and busy for him to hang around. Now that most of them were gone, he could walk around without getting in the way. The place was coming along nicely. He looked over at his foreman and friend, John Burch.

"It's looking like an office building." The old elementary school had been closed down for about ten years, since just after the new one had been built and opened. When he'd approached John about doing the work on it, he'd been a little skeptical. He had since changed his mind. "And the extra land out back is going to be perfect for parking, just like you said."

Tony replied, "Yeah, well I've been dreaming of owning this place for a while now, and moving things around in my head to make it work. The city would never sell it before. I have no idea how, but Garth worked it out with them." John nodded and walked him through some of the rooms he was going to use. "I have a guy coming in next month that will help with the surgery. I want it to be state of the art, and he'll know the right things I'll need. He was supposed to call you about dimensions."

"He did. We got the room all blocked off with strings. He said to have you come and look at it before we started." They moved into the room that had once been the library of the old building. "I thought about closing off the windows, but then I realized that this was in the courtyard that we're working on, and nobody can see in here but the dogs and cats. You don't like it we can block it off too."

"No, I love the idea. Natural light too." John said that was what he'd been thinking as well. "The courtyard; do you think that it'll need to be covered? I know that we talked about that."

The playground had been in terrible shape. Weeds were growing everywhere, trash had blown in from the streets, and the playground equipment had long since been removed because kids would still come around to play on it. It had been a dangerous place even when he'd been a kid. As the equipment began to rust, the hazards of playing on it increased. He thought the city had sold it all for scrap.

"Up to you. But if we cover only half of it, you'll have a place to have a nice quiet lunch; or the staff will. The animals don't care if it's raining or cold so long as they know they got someplace to come in from it. They might even like the openness, as well as some of the plants and things you got going in there, like you said." Tony decided to do that, leave half open; the rest, closest to the building, would be covered.

An hour later he was walking to the restaurant. Tony wasn't really sure what they were doing tonight. The place didn't even open for another month. And if it had been up to him, he would have told Elroy Baker to get lost. He wondered if anyone else had noticed that the man was a drunkard and screamed at his employees for no apparent reason. He would have thought Grandda would have; the man had been hanging out here for two weeks. But it wasn't his place, and Tony was going to stay out of it. For now, at least.

As soon as he opened the door and entered, Tony thought perhaps he'd been wrong about the man. He sure knew his shit if this was the first thing people saw when they walked in the door.

~~~

"It's lovely, isn't it?" Gracie watched Tony's reaction. He'd been the first to arrive, and she'd been waiting for someone to come and tell her what a lovely job they'd done. "The second chef called early this morning and asked if we'd like to do the front lobby for them. I had such a wonderful time with it that I was afraid that I'd gone overboard."

"It's spectacular." He moved closer to the display and smiled at her. "The faeries helped you with the feathers and such too, didn't they?"

"Yes. They thought that since it was a nice restaurant we should have a wonderful work in progress. Pip told me that if we did something that we would have to switch out all the time it would be time consuming. This way we can come and just take out the flowers that need replaced per season." She looked at the bright red tulips and pink pansies arranged in a heart motif. "They're set to open Valentine's Day weekend, so this is sort of a trial run for it."

The feathers that Tony noticed first had been used as leaves on the fake tree. It was really a large log that had been cleaned by them and brought in, but it looked wonderful. There were also pinecones that had been painted an array of colors to look like zinnias, as well as a small water garden that had a couple of koi in it. The bench that had been set in front of it was there to not just keep people from walking in the little garden, but to take pictures by should they want. Tony was impressed, not just with the work that had been done, but also that someone would want this sort of thing in a restaurant. It was going to have people talking about this for weeks after they left. He just hoped the food was as good.

"Mom, this is beautiful. And if I was the owner of this place, I'd give you a bonus. This is going to attract people like nothing else will. I just hope the food is as good as this looks." She hoped so as well. Elroy had been a friend of theirs for a long time, and she wanted this to work for him. "When do the others arrive?"

Almost as if he had summoned them, the rest of the family walked in the door. She was glad when Tony pulled out his tie and put it on, as the rest of them were dressed up as well. Gracie loved seeing them all spit and polished, as Katie was fond of saying. It was another ten minutes before they were ready to be seated.

This was going to be a trial run for the place, a time when they could see what worked and what didn't in the kitchen. Howie had been telling her for days now that Bethany's granddaughter was a good addition to the team there, and had brought out the best in the two under chefs as well. She had a feeling that it was going to go as smoothly as the garden did out front.

When they were seated at the long table, the wait staff brought out long trencher like platters of food. The woman standing at the head of the table started talking as soon as the trays were passed around.

"My name is Tansy. I'm an under chef here at Baker's, and I'm in charge of your first course. I'd like to walk you through what you're about to start with this evening. Also, I'd like to thank you for doing this for us. We're excited to have you here." Everyone agreed that they too were glad to be here. "The appetizers are as follows. The wrapped cheeses are goat cheese. The first one is rolled in peppercorns, the next in herbs, and the last has been caramelized. There are crackers on the table for you to use. The second grouping is fried homemade ravioli. The trio that we'll serve is beef, cheese, and a tomato herb mixture. These will be served with toast points and marinara sauce." Gracie was sharing her tray with Pip, as she was sitting to her right, and they both thought the cheeses were wonderful, but the ravioli was amazing. "The last thing on the tray is spiced pita chips that have been made here, as well as kopanisti. Its dip is made from feta cheese, garlic, and pepperoncini. It does have a bit of a bite to it, but not too bad. It can be served warm or at room temperature, and we have found that we like it either way."

"Oh, now that I love. This is hot and very flavorful." Tansy told her that it was the combination of all the ingredients that had time to marinate overnight. "I love it. I like it all, but this is my favorite."

The next thing to come from the kitchen was a salad. Such a mundane title for something so good. There were fresh croutons, slices of red bell peppers, as well as crumbled feta on the wedge of lettuce that was crisp and fresh tasting. The house dressing was a little too much for her taste, but she was assured that there would be the regular choices too.

After that, the main course was brought out. There would be three of them. The first was a sliced grilled chicken that was served on a bed of what appeared to be green noodles—which turned out to be zucchini made to look like pasta—as well as grilled asparagus. There was a sauce too, but served in a small dish on the side that was given to each of them by some of the staff. Gracie could have eaten an entire dinner on just that alone.

She was glad that she'd been warned ahead of time that the portions were smaller than they would be serving in the restaurant. They were, to her way of thinking, very good sized portions, but the waitress, Anna this time, said that these were about half of what would be served. She looked over at Howie to ask his opinion, and he looked upset. Before she could ask him what was wrong, the next entrée was brought out.

"This is chicken cordon bleu with green beans and almonds. The chicken was marinated in a buttermilk dressing before being wrapped around sliced ham and baby lacy Swiss." The chicken was so tender that she was able to cut it with just her fork, and as juicy as any fruit she'd eaten. "We're working on getting in fresh green beans, but this time of year they're a little hard to find. The chef thinks that once we're established, we might be able to get things more readily. So for now we have steamed green beans instead of the grilled ones that we'd prefer."

The last one was a grilled beef. Not steak, she'd been told, but a marinated tenderloin that had been blaze grilled to have a nice crust on the outside, but was still rare in the middle. Potatoes had also been sliced in half, then grilled to have a crisp shell but a tender and tasty middle. There was more of the zucchini, but this time it was mixed with yellow squash and sliced red bell peppers.

Lastly they were served desserts. There were several to choose from, and they were all encouraged to take several to try. Her lemon tarts were there, with the candied lemon rinds, and she looked at Howie to ask him if he'd had anything to do with this. Immediately she knew that something had happened, and wanted to go to the only man she'd loved in her life, aside from her husband and sons, and ask him what he needed. He was upset and she didn't know why. It wasn't like him to not enjoy the food, and that alone alarmed her.

After things were cleared away for the final time, bread was brought out. Gracie wondered why it hadn't come with the meals, but Tansy came to explain. It was brilliant.

"We're going to serve bread with each meal, but tonight we wanted to make sure that you had no distractions about which one would be our signature bread. There are four to choose from. I'm not to tell you what they are; we're going to ask for your opinion when you're finished. The butter on the table is just that, creamed butter. Enjoy."

Gracie took the first slice off the tray and buttered it, but was distracted again by her father-in-law.

"Howie, what is it?" He just shook his head. "Come on now. This is your favorite pastime; what is wrong with the food?"

"Elroy isn't the chef." She started to ask him what he meant and he stood up. "If you'll excuse me for a moment, I have to check something out. I'll be back."

She looked around when no one said a word. Something was up and she wasn't sure what it was, but knew that Howie would get to the bottom of it, whatever it might be. When he returned with a young woman in tow, all her sons stood up. She was proud of them at that moment, but they had frightened the woman. And she was upset with Howie, almost as much as he seemed to be. Gracie stood up then and smiled at the woman before addressing her sons.

"Boys, please be seated." All of them sat but Tony. "You're frightening her; please have a seat until we get to the bottom of this."

"Grandda, step away from her. Please." No one moved when Tony spoke. "Grandda, please? I need for you to let her go and move away."

"All right, son. I understand you." When he moved away from the woman, Gracie watched Tony. He hadn't sat yet, but he didn't move either. "I want you all to meet Coleen Greer. She's Bethany's granddaughter, and the one that cooked this lovely meal for us."

"She cooked it?" Micah looked around, then back at the woman. "I thought you hired a man to cook for this place. I mean, this was fantastic, but I'm sort of confused. Wasn't this a place for Elroy to get himself together?"

"He's a drunk." When Coleen moved away from Howie, a low growl came from Tony. She must have heard it too because Coleen turned to him. "You have a problem with me, buddy? Because as of right now, I think I can take you on and come out on top. I've had it up to here with men treating me like shit and them coming out smelling like a fucking rose."

"I think you smell fantastic, if you want to know the truth. But I'm as confused as you are. I'm not sure what I'm supposed to do. My mate died ten years ago. And yet here you stand." Gracie looked from Tony to Coleen and got it. His mate. "And my mom doesn't appreciate that sort of language. You might want to curb that a bit."

Gracie wasn't sure what she found so funny at the moment,

but she started to laugh. Tony had a mate. Even after him telling her just the other night what had happened all those years ago, she'd still held out hope that someone was out there for her little boy. He looked as poleaxed as the woman did upset. All that Gracie could think about was that her son was going to be happy.

"I've been busting my ass for the last ten hours to make this dinner a success. Do you think that fucking bastard locked up in his office cared one bit? No, he didn't even come out here when one of the helpers got hurt. Just stayed in there and drank his bottle like it was mother's milk." She wiped at the tears, and Gracie wanted to hug her. "Then just as we were plating the desserts, he comes out and fucking fires me. Well, good, because I can't work like that."

Before anyone could say anything, she turned and left them all there. Tony watched her for several seconds, then followed. Gracie wanted to warn him to go gently, but that was something that she'd not have to tell this son; he was as gentle as a lamb. When Howie sat down, the big man, Elroy, came from the kitchen area and started talking. Gracie knew immediately who he was, and he was indeed drunk.

"Howie, that woman is a pain in the butt and I don't want her here. She just took over like she was in charge. I told her that we'd have to go over the menu before tonight, and before I knew it, she had the stuff bought and started cooking it. I just let her hang herself." Elroy sat and Howie told him to shut up. "Howie, I told you I was going to stop drinking. You have to believe me when I told you I did try. But she had me so messed up that I just was drinking a little to keep the edge off."

"You're a drunk. And worse than that, you aren't fit to be in a kitchen. That girl carried you. And had I not had that particular sauce she made just yesterday, I wouldn't have known either. That staff she had here? They never let on at all that you weren't back there just working up a storm like we all thought you were. Come to find out, you were sleeping it off while they worked around you." Howie shook his head as he continued. "I'm so disappointed in you, Elroy. I just want to leave you to your own devices."

"Howie, I miss my wife." Elroy sobbed then, his entire demeanor defeated looking. As the man sat there crying about why he'd let Coleen hang herself, all Gracie could think about was Tony and the young woman. Good heavens, he was going to have a chef living with him too, she thought.

Anthony

CHAPTER 5

Coleen stopped moving and turned to look at the man who had followed her. She didn't have a car and she'd forgotten her coat, but her anger was keeping her warm for now. He stopped when she did.

"What do you want? To ridicule me some more? Tell me what a fucking failure I am? And I swear to you, if you reprimand me again for my poor language, I will hurt you." He told her he wasn't going to. "Good. What do you want?"

"All sorts of things come to mind, but I think you really would hurt me if I suggested them." She wasn't sure, but Coleen thought that he might be right. "I'm Anthony Bentley. Everyone calls me Tony."

"Well, Mr. Bentley, I'm Coleen Greer, unemployed chef after only forty-eight hours working." She wanted to cry, but had given herself a stern talking to this morning when she realized that her eyes were puffy from bawling so much. He took off his jacket and handed it out to her. "No thanks. I'm going home."

"Take it, please. The cold air has made your nipples hard, and all I can think about is seeing if they're pink too." She jerked the jacket from him and put it over her breasts. "Thank you. Now I can think. Sort of. Christ, you're beautiful when you're pissed off."

"What is wrong with you?" He shook his head. "I mean, there is a perfectly good reason for me being out here in the cold. I just lost my job. You, however, have your entire family in there, and Mr. Bentley, Howie, owns the place. I'm pretty sure you're related to him." He told her how he was. "Grandfather. Figures. You look like him."

"Thank you." She wasn't sure what to do now and turned to walk home. "I have a car. I can take you where you want to go."

She stopped and he ran into her from behind. His hands curled around her waist and his breath burned into her neck when he nuzzled there. Coleen felt her heart rate triple and the pounding of it heated her skin. He kissed her then, and it was all she could do to jerk away from him.

"Don't do that. What are you doing kissing me like...? I didn't invite you to touch me. Stay away from me." He said nothing, but she watched as he adjusted his cock. It was thick and hard, and she wondered what it would feel like in her hand for all of a minute before she looked at his face again. "Go away."

"I can't. I'm your mate, and I need to be with you. Or, failing that, as close to you as you're going to allow. Do you know what being a mate means?" Coleen said she did. "Good, this makes things so much easier then."

66

"For who? You?" She huffed at him, something that she hated doing almost as much as she did crying. "I'm not going to be your sex slave, Mr. Bentley. I have to get my life back on some sort of track. It'll be wobbly and a wreck most of the time, but it's my life and the only thing that I have any control over. I have to find a job, a place to live, as well as pay money back to a man that is out of my life but left me burning at the stake."

"You'll call my grandda by his first name but not me? Why not?" She told him. "Oh, okay; will you please call me Tony? That way when you come for me, you won't have so much to say before you come again."

Coleen hit him. Not one of those girly hits that she'd seen on television, but she doubled up her fist and slammed it right at his nose. And when he slipped back on the icy sidewalk and onto his ass, she turned and left. Coleen had an idea he wasn't human so she knew he'd be fine, but right now she had to get somewhere that she could think. And with him standing so close, she knew that wasn't going to be an option.

She heard him coming and took off running. The sidewalks everywhere were treacherous, but she managed to keep her footing enough to keep going. But when he hit her from behind, taking her to the ground, she rolled to her back and stopped.

It wasn't him, however. It was a huge cat, black, with the most gorgeous spots she'd ever seen. And before she could think what a terrible idea it was to put her hand anywhere near his mouth, Coleen ran her hand down his head to his back.

His forehead dropped to hers, and she realized then how large he was. But he wasn't hurting her. Coleen wanted to curl into his warmth, to let someone be the adult for a little while so she could crawl into a corner and suck her thumb. But she was an adult and she had responsibilities. And none of them were going to be solved by having another man in her life.

"Please get off me." He didn't move. "Please. I've had a really shitty day, and I want you to get off me so I can go home and try to gather up my dignity."

The panther lifted his head and looked to his right. Coleen looked in the same direction he did and saw two men that had been sitting at the table. One of them was Howie, the other was related to the man on top of her...brother probably. She asked them to tell him to get off.

"He can understand you. Called us out here to talk for him. He said to tell you he can shift, but he'd be naked." Howie laughed and she wanted to hit him too. "He also wants you to know that he can read your mind, and that he'd rather you didn't hit me too. You hit him?"

"In the nose. I would like to get up. My backside is cold and I want to stand up." Howie said that she'd be fine. "Look, is this some sort of voyeur thing? If so, you can count me out. I don't much care for sex, and less to have people watching."

Howie looked shocked, and the other man just laughed. Coleen tried to knock the panther off her, but he licked her face and she smacked him on the nose. Would anything ever go right for her? Or would she be forever fucked over?

The other man crouched down so that they were nearly face to face. "I'm Micah, his older brother. And the leader of this leap. Tony is your mate; he said you understand what that means." She did and nodded. "Good. I'm only repeating what he said to me, so please don't hit me as well. He told me that if you let him bite you, he can talk to you and we can go back inside the warm restaurant."

"And you're not fired." She looked at Howie when he spoke. "I'd be a fool to fire you. And I'm not gonna. I've also taken it upon myself to make sure that Elroy gets some help. You'll have to come and work the restaurant; there ain't nobody else to do it."

"Oh good. I'm the default cook. So much better than being fired." Howie said that he'd not meant it like that. "I know. But if you only knew.... Never mind. Just tell this idiot that he is not going to bite me, and if he doesn't get the fuck off me, I'm going to…well, I'll tell his mother."

He jumped off her so quickly that she thought someone had knocked him off. When she caught her breath, she stood up and brushed the snow off, careful to keep his jacket closed. When she turned to the three of them, two men and a big cat, Coleen decided that enough was enough.

"I read about this mate thing and then asked someone I know about it. It involves sex and the exchange of blood to be binding, right?" Micah nodded and told her that was right. "We've done neither and we never will. And if he tries, I will hurt him. I understand that I'm not supposed to be able to— and *supposed to* are the operative words there—hurt him, but I will do my damnedest to do so. I have enough shit going on in my life, and I don't need some macho shithead trying to help me. I can take care of myself."

"He needs to help you." She shook her head at Micah, then looked at Tony. "Coleen, no matter how hard you try to not let this work, he's going to try harder to make you see it his way.

It's what we do."

"Then he's shit out of luck. I just can't handle any more at the moment. I've had enough. Don't you think?" She turned and walked home. The tears fell then, useless and painful, but she knew that this was the only way that she'd not bring someone else into her crappy life.

Slipping into the house, she made it to her room without anyone seeing her. It was not that she wasn't glad that they were there, but they'd ask questions, and right now she didn't have any answers.

There was mail addressed to her sitting on the bed. Coleen just picked it up in her hand and without opening it, laid down.

Micky had ruined her life. Her life hadn't been as perfect as she wanted it to be up until he came into it, but it had been better than those of most of the people she'd worked with. She'd not had many friends, and fewer dates than others she knew, but she was content. Her plans to come to Ohio someday to meet up with her brother and grandma had been a plan, but nothing that she was going to stress over. Sheppard and she were close—they'd been all each other had at one time—but she knew that he had his own life and she had hers.

The knock at her door startled her from her dark thoughts. Coleen got up to open it and saw her brother standing there, with Tony behind him. When she said nothing, Sheppard walked away and Tony just stood there. It was tempting to close the door in his face, but she was afraid that he'd just break it down.

"I'd like to talk to you. And for the record, I wouldn't leave, but I also wouldn't break the door down." She told him to stay out of her head. "Then talk to me. I can't fix what I don't know about."

"I didn't ask you to fix anything. In fact, I think I made it clear that I didn't want you around." Her grandma cleared her throat and reminded her that Mandy was asleep. She lowered her voice but didn't change her mind. "Why don't you just go away, Mr. Bentley? I really don't have the energy to deal with you."

Instead of leaving he moved into her room, pushing her back enough that he could close the door behind him. Coleen sat down on the bed and he stayed at the door. The bills, still in her hand, drew her attention. She opened the first one.

"This one says that I owe forty-four dollars for Micky from three years ago. I didn't even know him then." She opened the next one. "Seventy-six dollars for an unpaid credit card that he had ten years ago. Because the courts decided that I'm responsible for Micky's bills, every fucking bastard in the world is trying to get a little more of me."

"You're not responsible for the ones that were made before you were married to him. They're sending those to you in the hopes of you thinking just what you did, that you have to pay them as well. I'm betting that a few that you get aren't even real." She laid back on the bed and said nothing to him. "Joey, my brother, is an attorney, and he's looking into this for you."

"I can't afford him." He said nothing. "And if you tell me he won't be charging me, then I won't believe you. No one does something for nothing. Well, I guess that's not true. My last attorney was free. But that didn't do me any good either, did it?"

"Micky fucked you over." She snorted at him. "I know that you know what he did to you, but what you don't know is that when he forged your names to those credit cards and loans, he committed fraud." She told him the attorney said it was viable because they were married at the time. "No, that's not true. He still has to have your permission to open a line of credit with your name on it."

Coleen sat up. "No, I was told that he could do that because since I married him, we were together in all things."

"Not if your name was forged." Coleen told him she had pointed that out to her attorney, and he'd said that she was responsible. "Joey wants to know how much effort you put into things when you know you're not going to be paid for them. And so you know, I told him you'd put in just as much as you would if you were getting paid."

"Yes, I would." There was no room for her to walk around, but she felt stupid for being on the bed. "I'd really like to go outside. If you want to go home, then that's fine. I really don't want anything to do with you. I thank you for the advice, but I'm really in no mood to be dealing with you. Not that I can afford to have this looked into any deeper, but it makes me feel better knowing that I'm not going to have to pay for every little thing he did."

"Grandda said to tell you that you can have the restaurant. He said that Elroy left tonight in a huff, saying that if Grandda was going to make that kind of demand on him, he was finished and wanted nothing to do with him. Grandda said that he'd pay you the salary that he was paying Elroy, with a percentage of the profits."

"That's very generous of him. Very. The courts are going to take half of my check no matter what I make, but the extra would be nice." She got up and pulled her jacket out of the tiny closet she had. "I'm taking a walk. I can't be here with you. Even before you got here and filled it up more, the room is too small for pacing."

~~~

Tony wasn't hurt that she didn't want to be with him. He understood completely that she was in over her head and drowning. But instead of going home, he followed Coleen, watching her. The need to help her, to take over, was making his cat a little antsy.

I just got off the phone with her attorney. He's a jackass. And since she left town without giving him any kind of repayment after he'd worked for her, he is having his firm send her a bill for the little effort — his words, not mine — the effort he put into her case. I think the little pisser wanted her to be so grateful for what he'd done that she'd let him fuck her. I think he did anyway. Tony asked how much the bill was. *Don't know, but I'm having it sent here. I told him that I was taking over as her representation. And guess what? He's heard of me. And was very impressed too.*

Everyone knows of the great and powerful Joseph Bentley. His brother laughed. *She has several bills at her house that are demanding money. Two of them, the ones she opened while I was there, are things from before she met this Greer person. I sort of fibbed when I told her you and I talked, and that you said she wasn't responsible for them because they didn't know each other at the time.*

It's true. Tony felt better then. *I'll have to see them, but I can make sure that she doesn't get any more shit like that from anyone. A few might slip by, but we can take care that the majority of them stop. Where is she going to be staying?*

I don't know. Right now she and I are walking. Not together, but I'm following her. She talks to herself too. Tony listened in a little, but knew that if she would speak to him, she could just turn and do so. *Also, tell Grandda that he has to pay her what he was paying Elroy. I had no idea that they were going to be taking half of what she makes to pay outstanding debts from this bastard. Tell him I'll pay the difference.*

Another fib, little brother? Not a good way to start out a relationship, Tony, lying to your mate. But I can understand why you did it. I'll talk to Grandda in a minute. I need for you to get her to gather up all her bills from this jerk and let me have a look at them. He asked him why. *Because, dear brother, she's related to me now, and I have to make sure that she's being taken care of. Just as you do.*

She keeps shoving me away. I'm not sure what to do. Tony watched her enter the diner and moved in behind her. *I think she's job hunting.*

I'll have Grandda call her now. As to what to do, just do what you are doing. Let her move through this at her own pace. She's hurt and scared. Tony sat across from her at a booth. *Go easy, but firmly. She'll come around.*

"What is it you want now?" Tony closed the connection between him and his brother when Coleen spoke to him. He said he was hungry too. "I'm not buying you dinner. Go to your house and make something. I'm sure that you have this big house with a kitchen to die for. Do you even cook?"

"I have a beautiful kitchen. Everything a cook would want to use. I haven't the slightest idea how to make some of it work.

Daniel, he's the guy that runs my house, he doesn't cook either unless you count a sandwich he slaps together." He ordered them both cheeseburgers and fries when one of the staff came to ask what they needed. "What if I had you come out, see the kitchen, and you can tell me how it works?"

"Do you suppose I'm stupid? That I'd just say, sure, I'd love to go to your house, you being a stranger and all? Will you be locking me in the basement too? Or do you have a shed for that sort of thing?" He shook his head and smiled at her. "And what if I don't want a burger and fries?"

"You do, remember? The mind thing." She started to get up and he held her hand in his. "Please don't leave me. I'm trying to get to know you. Let's just have a nice dinner, talk a little, and you can tell me about your plans for the restaurant." Almost on cue her cell phone rang.

While she talked to his grandda he watched her. She was cautious, and while he knew why, he still found it interesting that she didn't jump on the chance to take over the restaurant, even knowing that the money was going to be good. Nor did she just roll over to Grandda, something else that really impressed him. Grandda was used to getting his way, and Tony wondered how this was setting with him. When she put down the phone, he could tell she was excited but holding back.

"Your grandfather said that he'd give me the job that he'd given Elroy, and said that he'd pay me a percentage of the profits too, more than he would have given me before. All in cash. Baker needs some serious help, but he has to want it. Your grandda can't bully him into wanting to get better." Tony agreed with her. When two glasses of tea were bought to them, she shoved hers away. "I don't care for tea. It's bitter and usually dry tasting. Can I have water?"

"The tea container is cleaned nightly here, and it's brewed fresh every day. Try it. If you don't like it, you can certainly have whatever you want." She sipped it, and he could tell by the surprised look on her face that she thought it was good. "My sister-in-law, Rylee, owns this place. Mostly they cater to the local vets and homeless, but everyone comes here at some point in the day. Even to just catch up on gossip. One of the vets runs the kitchen, and most of the staff is from the shelter. They're trying to work at getting something other than homeless on their resumes."

"Grandma told me that your brother puts them together for them—their resumes—and helps them get to and from jobs to help out. I guess you're pretty wealthy." He nodded; there was no point in keeping it from her. It would be hers as well soon enough. "I'm broke. I mean, deep in a dark hole never to see the light of day, broke."

"If you're trying to make a point, I don't get it. Yes, you're having some financial difficulties right now, but we can work around that. By the way, Joey talked to that attorney of yours, and he thinks he's an idiot. Joey wants to know if you have all the bills that supposedly are in your ex-husband's name, as well as any other records you might have. He'll look into them."

She said nothing as their food was set in front of them, except to ask for barbeque sauce for her fries. "I don't want your brother doing anything for you because he thinks it will pave the way for you to get what you want." He said that he wasn't. "Sure he isn't. And this other attorney; what makes him think that Harry didn't do his best? I'm not saying that he did, but why does Joey think this?"

"The attorney wanted you to sleep with him because you were so grateful for him getting you the deal he did." Tony poured catsup all over his fries, and looked up at her when she said nothing. "What? You didn't know that?"

"He's married." Tony asked her what that had to do with it. "I don't know. I guess I figured.... Your brother, he can read minds too? Over the phone?"

"No, but he called this Harry person, and I guess because of what he is, no one can lie to him." She asked him what his brother was. "Chris, his wife, is the grand witch. So Joey, being a cat, is her familiar."

"You're kidding me." He said that he wasn't, and watched her dip five frics in the sauce before shoving them in her mouth. When she was done chewing, she picked up her burger in both hands and continued. "So you have a witch and cats in your family. That's gotta be weird."

"Also a faerie. Pip, Burke's wife, is a faerie. He is too, by the way. Also, two of my brothers, Nolan and Burke, are doctors, and Joey is an attorney. I'm a veterinarian for small animals, and working my way up into being a surgeon for them as well. And you met Micah; he's the leader of our leap because he killed the other one when he tried to hurt his wife, Reggie." Tony pushed the burger to her mouth when she stared at him. After she took a healthy bite, he continued. "My nephew, Shane, has a dragon that protects him. He's attached to him somehow, and will show himself when Shane turns thirteen. I think that's sometime in the summer."

"Why are you telling me all this?" He said she needed to know. "For what reason? I told you, we're not going to be together. I don't want you in my life."

"Well, that's really too bad. You're there now, and even though I'd like nothing better than to take you home, strip you down, and make love to you, I also know that you've been hurt before, and I'm not going to rush you." Coleen said nothing as she ate the rest of her burger. "I would very much like for you to come and see our home. It's a work in progress right now. I'm trying to make it seem less cold and more homey, but I'm not having any luck. Mom tried to help, but I think, as she said, it needs a woman's touch."

"I wouldn't have the slightest idea how to make a place homey. The kitchen I could help you with, but I know what I like." She ate the rest of her fries and then ordered a piece of cherry pie with ice cream. "This isn't going to work. People will wonder why you are dating beneath you."

"I don't want to date you. I want to marry you. I have no idea how you think that I'd be marrying beneath myself. As far as I'm concerned, we're going to be equals in all ways." He watched her face. "And I have to tell you, I'm so happy right now that you're not one of those picky, only eating a wee bit sort of women. It's great to see someone who knows what they want and has it."

"I love food." He asked her about the food here. "It's fresh and well made. The burgers are done without being dry. The tomatoes taste fresh, and that's a wonderful thing for this time of year. I'd put the mayo on the side if I were them, ask for cheese choices, and I'd not change a thing about the bun. The fries are made from potatoes, not taken from a bag of frozen shit, and the barbeque sauce is homemade too."

He laughed. "I tasted a really good burger with some good salty fries. And my pie, apple, not cherry, was really good too. But then I know who baked it and where the cherries came from."

"The fries needed to have sea salt on them." He grinned at her. "Why are you doing this? Being nice to me?"

"Because I'm a nice guy." He leaned back on the seat and looked at her. "I'm a panther, you know that, but I never thought I'd find a mate…or at least find one again. There was someone, long ago, but she was murdered and I thought that I'd be alone for the rest of my days. Finding you makes me want to do this right, to make it perfect. I've been given a great gift, and I don't want to fuck it up."

"Pretty words, Anthony, but I'm not very trusting. Not any longer." He nodded, telling her he understood. "Micky wasn't right in the head. It took me a bit to figure that out, but by then it was too late. He wasn't crucl, not harshly so. It wasn't like he tied me down and raped me, but he did knock me around a little to get me to understand what he thought was perfectly all right. I might not have a lot going on, then or now, but there are things I just won't do, like cheat."

"I don't want you to cheat either. And I've no use for men who beat women. I would like for you to give this a chance. You might find that you like me. A little anyway." She sat there, and he could see her sadness. "Would you like to see my house? Really, I would like for you to take apart my kitchen and make it your own."

"I'm not living with you either. I want my own house with my own things in it. Things that are soft when I sit on them, a television that gets more than two channels because it only works by the remote that was lost. I could have had those things before Micky, but I was saving for bigger. For me." He could tell she was torn, that she did want to go and see it. "If I go to your house, you'll take me home when I want to go?"

"Yes." He would too, no matter how much he wanted her to stay with him. "I swear to you on my mom's life. Or mine if she finds out that I lied to you in any way. My mom loves me, but she'd beat me within an inch of my life if I hurt you."

"All right, but nothing is going to happen." She pushed her dessert plate away and looked around the diner. "I can't let you into my life and heart. I don't want to have to hurt anyone because you find out I'm not worth it."

"That will never happen, Coleen. As far as I'm concerned, you're already in my life. I just have to convince you of that."

He paid the bill and then left a hefty tip. She nodded as if she approved and they left. Tony was as nervous as he'd ever been. His mate was going to his house.

CHAPTER 6

She didn't have any idea what she had expected, but the mansion that he pulled up in front of would never have entered her mind. Coleen supposed she thought of him having a bachelor pad or a one level house. He opened the door for her and she got out and stared.

"It's really big." He said that he'd had little to do with it, as the under witch had done it. "An under witch? I'm supposing you mean someone that works with Chris."

"Yes, her name is Myra. And to warn you, she is very bright." She wondered why he'd said that when he explained. "I mean she dresses brightly. From head to toe. At Christmas she had decorated trees and candy canes all over her. Even her hair. She's a wonderful woman, but a little much sometimes in her mode of dress."

They moved into the main part of the house and she backed up when a very tall, lanky man came to greet them and said his name was Daniel. He also looked flustered, and he was covered in bits of flowers. She asked him what was wrong.

"The faeries, my lady. They are…well, they're…. Perhaps it would be best if you came to see. I'm not sure that the kitchen will be the same." She followed the two men as Tony introduced her to him. "My lady, I'm sorry for you to see us at our worst. We usually get along well, but for some reason, I think they got it in their heads to make something."

The kitchen seemed to have exploded. Not any of the many and varied pieces of equipment, but everything was covered in flower pieces. And standing in the middle of it all were the tiniest people she'd ever seen. Coleen walked slowly to them, almost afraid that they'd take off if she startled them too much.

"Did you two do all of this?" The blue one looked at the yellow one before nodding at her. "I see. And what is it you were trying to do? Because I can't tell if you were trying to make a mess or you were having a flower fight."

"I knew you were coming." The blue one shoved at the yellow one when it spoke. "I did too. I told you yesterday morn that we were to meet the new lady of the house. You told me I was full of dung."

"You said that we were meeting a stranger. I pointed out that until we met someone, everyone was a stranger. Then you hit me. Like you always do when you know that I'm right. Which I have to tell you is a lot more than you —" Coleen snapped her fingers and they both looked at her. "Well, she doesn't. I'm very smart and she knows it."

"I'm sure you are, but first things first. I'm Coleen." They introduced themselves. "All right, Gom and Awnia. What do you suppose should be done about this mess you've made? And so you know, I'm not sure how you thought I was coming, but for now, we'll table that. But this is a mess, and it's not going to be cleaned up on its own."

"We must clean it up." Coleen nodded at Gom, the blue faerie. "You're very beautiful, my lady."

"There will be no sucking up either. You made a mess, and it's to be cleaned up by the two of you. I came here to have a look at this kitchen, and so far, I'm not impressed." She looked at Tony and Daniel before looking back at the little people and continuing. "How long will it take you to get this back to the way it was?"

"Not long." Awnia looked like she was going to argue with Gom some more, but Coleen only snapped her fingers again. "Yes, we'll have it cleaned in a minute. But you should know that I did know you were coming."

"Clean. Then we'll have a look at the kitchen, all right?" Coleen turned her back on the two little people and looked at Daniel. "I'm just here to look at the kitchen, but since they made a mess, do you think you could show me around the rest of the place? It's a lovely home."

"Thank you, my lady. It is a lovely home. Still a might under furnished, but I think it's coming along now." She followed Daniel out of the kitchen and into the dining room. "Just this morning this room had no table and there were no dishes…I don't believe there were cabinets in this room either. You might have thought of it. It's going to be nice when all of the family comes now."

"Thought of it?" She looked at Tony for an explanation, but he was laughing so she ignored him for now. "When I was working my way through college, there was this home that some of us would go and cook for when they entertained. The lady of the house had deep cabinets in her dining room that held all the extra plates and silverware. She had this amazing pantry too, stuffed full of things that we'd get to use. Most of them weren't modern, but they were beautiful to use."

"I'm sure you'll find them here as well." Coleen followed him to the living room then, Tony lagging behind, still laughing. Daniel pointed to the fireplace. "The mantel is a nice touch. Thank you for that. As well as the doors on either side. Much nicer for bringing in the wood. Oh, wait, it's gas. Very good, ma'am."

Coleen looked at Tony. "Explain. And so you know, there is a lot of it you have to do. First of all, why you are nearly falling over from laughter? And why does Mr. Daniel seem to think I'm the one that turned the fire to gas, and chose the cabinets in the dining room?"

Tony looked at Daniel and he disappeared back into the kitchen area. Tony came toward her and she wanted to back away. But she stood her ground until he put his hand over her eyes.

"Do you like the couch in this room? Or would you prefer something like a sectional? I have no preference so you know, just comfy." She pulled his hand down and he put it back. "Trust me for a moment."

"I don't trust you at all, but you'd better have a good reason for this. I like comfy too. But not a sectional. When one part of it goes bad, then you have an entire thing to replace or fix. I like the smaller versions of couches, love seats I guess, and comfy shareable chairs." He asked her what colors they would be.

"Earth tones. With reds and blues. But not bright like spring, more of an autumn sort of color. And some print, but not a lot."

He pulled his hand from her face and turned her to the living room. Coleen looked at the furniture there, all if it just like she had described. The throw pillows were covered in a pretty print, and the couches, three of them, circled the fireplace. Chairs were here and there, and their material looked like a soft brushed denim. When her knees felt a little wobbly, he held her to his body until she was able to stand again.

"The house is magical, as I told you." She nodded and thought of lamps, and they appeared. "You keep that up and you're going to have the entire house filled beautifully. What would you do to the bedroom? A big bed? Right now I have a four poster bed, with a thick mattress. I'd like to take you up there now and show it to you."

She clung to him. Coleen wasn't sure if she was terrified or in awe of the house. But the moment that Tony turned her into his arms, all thoughts of houses and lamps seemed to just disappear. And when he lowered his head to hers, slowly so that she could no doubt tell him to stop, Coleen wanted him to kiss her.

His kiss was gentle. Just a small brush of his lips over hers. And when he stared at her, looking deeply into her eyes, all she could think about was what it would be like to have him make love to her.

"Not to you. But with you. I want to make love with you, Coleen." She nodded. "Are you saying you agree or that you want me as well? I won't rush you. But I don't want you to say later that I forced you. You have to want this as much as I do."

He was giving her the option. She didn't know what she wanted, if she was honest. And with herself, she seldom was anything but honest. Her licking her lips had him moaning, but he didn't pull her to him nor push the issue.

"I have so much baggage. Getting involved with you... aren't you afraid of me bringing you down to my level? What if they come after you? Want you to start paying   these things?" He brushed his mouth over hers again. "When you do that, all I can think about is being naked with you. Feeling your hands on my body. Your mouth touching me in places that are wet and hot."

"I want that as well."

He kissed her this time, deep and long, his tongue dueling with hers in the most delicious ways. And when he pulled her to his body, groin to groin, breast to breast, she felt his cock swell against her and she moaned. He took her hand in his and moved it down his body to his cock. And when she cupped him in her palm, he rocked into her until she wanted to tear his pants open and see him.

"I need you." He lifted her up in his arms and carried her out of the room. They were nearly up the stairs when he kissed her again, this time leaving no doubt of his need for her. Going up them once again, she pulled at the buttons on his shirt, tugged it down enough that she could taste his flesh. They had no more than crossed over the threshold then she was on the bed.

"This is forever." She nodded, sitting up to pull her clothing off. Her blouse hit the floor; her bra, barely open, was shoved up over her breasts, and he was there suckling them. "Christ, I need you."

"Please. Hurry." He stood up, then knelt down again and pushed her breasts together. Suckling at the tip of one, then the other, he had her so close that she slid her hand down to her pussy to get some relief. He stood up then and pulled her up from the bed.

"I can't wait." He tore her things off her; her bra was ruined, her pants seemed to have been torn at the seams and were piled near the rest of her clothing. When he cupped her ass he stretched out his hands. She heard the silk of her underwear tear and it made her pussy hotter, her juices gush from her. Soon she was standing before him in nothing but a pair of socks. "Beautiful. But don't run."

He was gone. Just like that, the cat stood before her, and the man she wanted was gone. The cat's head seemed larger than before, his body sleeker. And when he nudged her back, she fell to the bed and cried out when he slid his massive head between her legs and licked her pussy.

His tongue was rough, but soft too. And when he touched it over her clit Coleen came twice more, her body bowing up off the bed with a scream spilling from her lips. His teeth nipped at her pussy, her thighs, and her hips. Everywhere he touched her, every small hurt he made, the cat licked it away, the feel of his tongue like a cock as he lapped at her pussy.

Come for him. The voice in her head, Tony's voice, brought her again and again. Coleen cupped her breasts, pulled at her painfully needy nipples until she was sure they were going to be sore later. And when she felt the room tighten, she looked down her body to see Tony there, his mouth just a scant inch from her clit.

"To see you like this, laid out like a feast for me, all I can think about is that you're mine." She wanted to deny it, tell him it was just sex, but Coleen wasn't stupid. This was it; this was the bonding and mating of two people meant for each other. "When I fuck you, and I will, I'm going to take your throat, bite you deep, and then take your blood into my body. As soon as I do that, you belong to me. No other male will touch what is mine. Do you understand me?"

"Yes."

He leaned to her pussy and blew gently over it. She was so sensitive that she came again, screaming out his name even as he suckled her clit into his mouth and bit down. Coleen came so many times after that that she knew she was going to die. And what a way to go. But even when she thought she'd had enough, that there wasn't a thing left in her to give him, he'd do something else, touch her in a way that would have her crying out his name while holding him to her.

He moved up her body then, his mouth nipping and biting much like his counterpart had. The tiny wounds were never painful to the point she wanted him to stop; on the contrary, they were sexy, erotic, and made her come a dozen more times. When he took her nipple in his mouth, he watched her, his eyes locking onto hers as if he were looking into her, deep within her very soul. He was, her mind told her...he was looking at her like none other had before. And he didn't find her lacking.

His cock touched her clit and she waited for the pain of it. He was thick, longer than any other man she'd been with, and she knew he was going to hurt her. But instead he slid slowly into her, back and forth, in and out, until she wrapped her legs around his calves and pulled him to her. As soon as he was buried into her as deeply as she thought he could go, he pushed harder, bringing her over the edge again until she was dizzy with it.

"I'll never harm you; do you know that?" Yes, she told him, she knew. "Feeling you wrapped around me, it's like nothing I've ever felt before. My mate, my mind keeps telling my heart, and I've fallen in love with you."

He moved then, pulling out slowly and moving back into her just as slowly. She hurt, she needed to come so badly, which was surprising after so many releases. But he never stopped watching her face, never slowed or hurried through making love to her. Cupping her breast, he thumbed her nipple until she was ready to beg him to fill her, to give her the climax that she knew would be powerful, fulfilling like none before.

"Come."

The one word tore her asunder, and she screamed out his name, holding onto his shoulders so that she'd not fly away. And his second command to come brought her again, this time making her vision blur, her body burn with something so powerful that she felt her breath hitch and her heart stop for a second. As soon as his mouth touched the pulse at her throat, she tilted her head and gave him all that was her. His bite, his tearing into her throat, gave her such a rush that when he came with her, all she could think about was that he was hers.

~~~

Tony held her in his arms until he thought he could move without dying. Christ, he'd never been so blown apart by having

89

sex with a woman. He supposed it had a great deal to do with the fact that she was his mate, but he could hardly move. When he did, he rolled to his back, taking her with him, and reached for the blanket beside them to wrap up in.

His heart was pounding a thousand beats a second. His body felt relaxed, almost putty like. Running his hands up her back then down again had him grinning. She was his, now and forever. When she stirred, he stilled his hands, not wanting to wake her just yet. Tony wanted to bask in the afterglow of having a mate. He was worried she'd be upset.

"I'm not." He looked at her when she lifted her head and looked down at him. Tony kissed her, a quick touch of his mouth to hers. "I can read your mind, feel your thoughts and emotions. Because we had sex?"

"Some of it. There is the magic that I was telling you about. All of us share it for the most part. And our mates and children that we bring into our heart and home do as well." They both looked around the room. "There was only a single dresser in here before, and…" She put her hand over his mouth. He ran his tongue over her palm until she moved her hand. "You're going to have to get used to it sooner rather than later. When we get up from this bed and head to the shower to make love there, the bed will make itself and all of our clothing will be gone."

"I don't have anything here to wear. *Someone* tore it to shreds." He grinned, feeling entirely too happy to care about a pair of pants and a shirt. "What do you propose I wear home?"

"You are home." She stiffened a little but said nothing. "I know this is really quick and scary, but trust me, we're going to

90

be just fine. And as far as you bringing a lot of baggage to this relationship, it's going to work out as well. Joey is on the case."

"Joey isn't going to find anything but what the other guy did. Right? I mean, he worked hard for me, even though it was for free." Tony kissed her again, rolling her to her back as he rocked into her. "Sex won't fix everything either."

"No, but it is a nice distraction." He rocked into her over and over, loving the way her face tightened up, her eyes darkened with desire. "I could easily come again. Fill you with my cum while you scream out my name. I love the way your breath catches when you're close, the way your nipples tighten up when I touch them."

"You're going to make me come again." He told her he hoped so. "Tony, we need to talk. I mean, you need to know how much – Oh God, yes!"

He suckled at her nipple hard, nibbling on it as he held her to him, her ass fitting firmly into his hand. When he took her harder, fucking her with just enough power to take him over the edge with her, he offered her his throat and cried out when she bit down on his flesh there. Tony wanted her to taste him, take his blood into her body so that she'd be one with him. Pulling his cat a little, he cut at his throat and pulled her head to the wound he'd made. The moment she took him into her body Tony came hard when she did, empting into her only to fill and do it again.

This time when he dropped over her, he rolled at the same time. She was limp on his body, her face relaxed in slumber. Moving her carefully, he got up from the bed and moved to pull on his jeans. He needed to talk to his brother and he didn't want to be distracted if she woke up. Tony wanted to know where Joey was on all of this. He called him on the phone rather than reach out to him this time.

"She's been fucked." Tony wanted to say she had, but knew that his brother hadn't meant that literally. "I had her attorney send me all that he had on the case. Which I might add he didn't want to do. Still hoping, I guess, for her to come to him. Anyway, there are bills here that don't even have her name on them. Nor her ex-husband's. I mean, it's like they went out and found a shitload of unpaid bills from companies and decided to get payment on them. I've looked into a couple of these businesses. One of them is really upscale furniture—nothing this man seemed to be able to afford—and the other one doesn't exist. Nor has it ever as far as I can find. This one that I'm looking at right now, it has no social security number on it, no address that's even in the same state, and it looks like it had a four-hundred-dollar limit on it; yet it seems to have been charged up over six grand. Something is wrong with all of this. I have another one here that doesn't even have a dollar amount owed on it. It just had a circle around where the billing is, and the word 'whatever' written there. And when I compare it to the paperwork that was given to the judge, it says ten grand. What the fuck were they doing?"

"This lawyer that sent you this stuff, did he do so because of your magic, or was he being a nice guy?" Joey said he'd had to make him. Then he asked Tony why they'd do this in the first place. "I don't know. But do you suppose this is something that this firm that he works for does a lot of? Find a person who died and hose them for whatever they can get out of them?

She's supposed to make payments to the firm, right? And they distribute the money. Isn't that what you told me?"

"It is. Let me look here for a second. Hang on." Tony headed to the kitchen and saw that some improvements had been done here, as well as it being spotless. He asked Daniel if he knew how to use any of these new items.

"I'm afraid I do not, sir. There is a tea maker that I have put to good use. The instructions for it were very clear. And then there is the pantry. I wasn't aware that the young madam was a cook." Tony went to have a look. He remembered Coleen mentioning that she'd seen some older pieces in someone's house, and now they had them as well. The pantry was also larger than his living room at his old place, as well as boasting a huge walk-in freezer. It, like the pantry shelves, was full. "She'll know how to use these things, I'm thinking. I have to admit, I'm very glad that you're not going to have to depend on me to feed you using these items. They're quite out of my league."

"Yes. And you should taste her cooking, Daniel. I'm hoping that she'll be running the new restaurant in town too." Daniel made him another thick sandwich, this time of turkey instead of roast beef. It was still a few hours until morning, so he figured that either they'd go get something for breakfast…or maybe Coleen would cook for them.

"Clothing. She's going to need to get something else to wear." Daniel nodded and moved to a door that he didn't remember from before. When he opened it, Tony could see a washer and dryer, as well as a full basket of what he thought was not his clothing. There had been a mudroom of sorts, but this was obviously a place to take care of their clothing. Even a sewing machine sat with an ironing board and iron.

"They arrived while we were having a dusting in the kitchen. Things for the young miss that I was going to take up to your room, but decided to wait." Nodding, Tony told him that was a good idea. "Very good, sir."

He heard his brother laughing before he spoke to him again. "All right. You could be onto something. I'm going to have to take a trip out there to see what I can find and have it turned over to me. Also, I'd like to talk to the judge in all of this. I don't believe that he's in on this—I have no idea why—but I'd like to talk to him. Perhaps we can get this taken care of quickly for her." Tony thanked him. "How are things going there? Is she all right with the house and everything?"

"The magic, you mean? I'm not sure. She knows that it changes; even living here the last few weeks I'm still a little freaked out by it, but she took it okay." Joey said it could take anyone some getting used to. "I don't think I've ever been so consumed by a person before. In a good way, I mean."

"I know what you mean. It's like you can't think what it's going to be like having a mate, then when you get her in your life, you can't believe how amazing it is. Wait until you have a child. It changes everything." Tony had seen it happen to his other brother. Micah now had three kids, two girls and a little boy, and rather than seeming like he was overwhelmed by it, he was relaxed, funnier, and easier to talk to. "I'll let you know when I get ready to go out there. I want to take Chris to the casino too. Not to gamble, but to see it. It's a place you have to see to believe." He told him he'd talk to him later and sat down at the table to wait.

The ringing phone startled him as he ate his pre-breakfast, as he was calling it. Daniel too, apparently. But when he answered it, even from across the room he could hear that the person at the other end was upset. Daniel handed the phone to him when he heard his name. When he got Bethany to calm down enough to understand her, he asked her to repeat what she'd said.

"My sister is here. She's trying to take Mandy back to Florida with her." Tony asked her why. "Because she said that it was unfair of me to get the money when she'd done all the work. I'm not even sure what she means by that."

"Okay, I'm on my way." Tony grabbed up the basket of clothing to take with him to get Coleen. "Is she at the house now? If not, please don't let her in."

"I won't, but she's coming over. Sheppard isn't here either. He went job hunting this morning at a place in Cincinnati. He won't be back until tomorrow." Tony told her he was coming. "I don't know where Coleen is, do you?"

"She's with me. She and I will be there soon. Just don't let your sister in if you can help it. If you can't stop her, don't let her anywhere near Mandy. Even if you have to call the police." She said that she'd do that. "Okay, we'll be there soon."

Tony took the stairs two at a time and entered the bedroom just as Coleen was getting up. He told her quickly what was going on. As she pulled on a sweater and jeans that had been in the basket, he marveled at how well they fit her slim body, and she told him to focus.

"If I focus any harder, we're not leaving this room." With a huff she went to the bathroom and closed the door. The lock engaging had him laughing. As if a plank of wood would keep him from her. But they were in a hurry now.

CHAPTER 7

The house was quiet and there were no different cars out front, but Micah wasn't taking any chances that Carol might come in the back door. He'd locked it, but who knew with this woman. All he'd been asked to do was to wait there for Tony and to keep the occupants safe.

When Tony had asked him where he was a few minutes ago, it had been nothing for him to walk over to the little house and look around. He'd sent Bethany and Mandy to Faerie Tales and Dreams with Reggie and his children. No one was hurting his newest family members, not if he had anything to say about it.

We're here. Around back. When the door opened to his brother and Coleen, he smiled at them both. *Don't freak her out, okay? Just tell her what is going on with her grandma. I'm still laying the groundwork for us.*

You're bonded. Do I at least get to welcome her to the family? Tony said no, just to wait. *Everything okay? Anything —*

"Are you two talking about me?" Micah laughed and said

that they were. "Don't do that. Please. I'm fucking freaking out enough as it is with the house doing weird shit, and giving me clothing that is better than I would have picked out."

"You do look lovely." Coleen growled at him. "Christ, you're wonderful, and perfect for Tony. And yes, the house is a bit to get used to. My daughters have a faerie each, and our son will too soon, I guess."

The door rattled on its hinges when someone pounded on it. Micah started for the door, but Coleen beat him to it. He wasn't worried; if they had to, him or Tony, or both, could protect her. But when Coleen jerked the door open, Micah didn't think they'd have to. She was royally pissed off.

"Aunt Carol. What the fuck do you want? And so you know, if you try one bit of the shit you did to Sheppard or me when we were growing up, I will kill you where you stand." The woman started to move into the house, but Coleen stopped her. "You answer the question and I might see myself letting you in if you don't piss me off more. But I'm thinking the chances of that are slim to none, don't you think?"

"You always did have such a shitty opinion of me, and I can see that it's not gotten any better. Why, I have no idea, but you will respect me. Where is that child? I've decided that I want to keep her. I might have been a bit hasty in sending her to Beth. I'll just take her back with me, and you call up Sheppard and tell him I have her again." Coleen said no. "Then don't, I don't care, but I'm taking her with me. Beth is too old to take care of you and the child."

"Mandy." Carol looked confused. "Her name. It's Mandy, not the child. Or child. Mandy, short for Amanda. And you're not taking her anywhere. And if you try, I'll have you arrested so fast your head will spin."

"I don't believe I asked your permission." She started to shove her way by Coleen, and Micah felt his cat stir under his skin. But he wasn't sure if he was impressed by Coleen or trying to warn her. But again, Coleen had it under control and blocked her aunt from not just getting in the house, but even touching her. "Get out of my way, Coleen, or I'll have to resort to smacking you. You know that I will too. I don't care how old you've gotten."

"Hit me ever again and I will end your miserable life. I'm not five anymore." Carol backed up. It wasn't until then that Micah thought she saw him and Tony. Carol asked him what they were doing in this house. Coleen answered for him. "This is my future brother-in-law, Micah, and my future husband, Tony. Gentlemen, this is my aunt, Carol Lewis. She's probably one of the meanest—if not *the* meanest—people you will ever meet. But she won't be coming around much, and if she does, then we'll be having all our conversations with glass between us."

"Coleen, so help me, you're trying my patience. I want to take *Mandy* back with me." She said the name hard, viciously even. "Get her things gathered up and bring her to me if you won't let me in my own sister's home. I'm staying at what I guess they're considering a nice hotel. The place, like this one, is a dump. Bethany never did have any sense with money."

"Oh, I don't know. I own my house, while you rent yours. And I would imagine that you're behind in that too. What I don't understand, and perhaps you can clear it up for me, is why you're telling these nice people that it's your sister's house? You never have thought of me as your sister before, Carol; why now?" All of them turned to look at Bethany when she came into the room with them. Tony moved to stand next to Coleen, and Micah stayed by Bethany. "I cannot believe that you think I'd just hand that child over to you after the things she told me you did and said to her. You're not taking Mandy back with you, period. And if you so much as look like you're going to try, I will call myself an attorney and have him look into your life. I'm sure that you have a lot of skeletons in it that would make your life harder."

"You stay out of my life. What I've done before has no bearing on what I want now. Why did you have them take that money back from me? I'm supposing that you called Sheppard and told him to stop paying me to keep the child, didn't you?" Bethany nodded. "That money went a long way to helping me make ends meet. I didn't think you'd be smart enough to have known about the money, much less how to keep me from it. Maybe I won't take the child back if you call Sheppard up and tell him that I have her. That way you can raise her as you see fit, and I'll have the extra income. You don't need it anyway, what with Coleen here. She looks like she could turn a few tricks for you."

"If you want to talk to him yourself, you can wait until the morning. He's only gone job hunting." Bethany sat down on the couch and smiled at him. "Have a seat, Micah, this has been a long time in coming. Coleen, honey, you and that man of yours should sit too. Come in Carol, take a load off. You're probably exhausted from plotting and planning how to make an easy buck. You've been doing it since we were children."

Coleen moved back from the door and opened the screen door for her aunt. Micah could tell that Carol was confused, but not beaten yet. He was glad now that he was going to let this drama play out. When Carol was seated, Tony sat next to Coleen, and for all intents and purposes, they looked like a family gathering.

"Where is she?" Coleen asked her who. "The child, Mandy. Where is she? Or have you sold her off to pay your debts? It would be like you to do something underhanded like that."

"No, that would be you. You're the bitch that takes what she wants, and damn the person who had it first. And while I have debt, yes, I'm not a liar and a bitch about it. What have you done now to get you into hock, Carol? Have you gone gambling again? Are you in danger of being tossed out on your ass due to nonpayment of your rent? I guess having your gas turned off isn't such a hardship on you, living where it's fairly warm all the time. I remember once you tried to have Sheppard hide away so you could claim kidnappers took him from you. You hoped that the community would come to arms and raise the money for you to pay off the nonexistent kidnappers. Didn't work though, did it? Sheppard saw you for what you were before I did."

"Screw you. It would have worked had you just kept your mouth shut every time I tried to talk to the police. Why did you do it, Coleen? Were you jealous that I had the brains and you had nothing? But I'll tell you this, I should have beaten you more." Carol looked at Micah and then at Tony. "You're going to marry her? You should know that she doesn't work hard at keeping a marriage together. Her first husband, Micky Greer, he was good to her. But she just wouldn't play ball when he wanted her to. I never saw what the big deal was. So what if she took a little money that didn't belong to her. Everyone does it all the fucking time."

"No they don't. Just people like you and him." Coleen looked at Tony as she continued. "He wanted me to work the casino for him. Lie about how much he put down on the bet, and to cheat at cards for him. That's what pissed him off the most, I think, that I was nothing like Carol here." Bethany didn't know, and Micah was pretty sure that Tony was just finding out about that part himself. "Then one day he confessed to me that my dear Aunt Carol told him not just where I was, but had also given him the idea that I was a great deal like my mother. Another liar and cheat. It was another reason that I wanted out of his life. If he was like Carol, then he wasn't worth knowing."

"So? You didn't do what he wanted, did you? You're so squeaky clean that you make me sick. But he did get you in the end, didn't he? Fucked you over even from the grave." Coleen said nothing but just smiled. Micah would bet anything that this was a showdown long in the making. "What do you think you're going to be able to do now, Coleen? Work yourself to death until you get the money paid off? Sell off another home while you're at it? Poor little Coleen, lost it all over a man."

"Actually, she might not have to pay any of it back." Everyone turned to Tony when he spoke. "I'm having my brother look into a few things. And he's a really good attorney that will gladly represent either of these women should you have to be put down. And I say it like that because that's how we deal with animals that have gone bad. We don't kill them so much as put them out of their misery. I just thought you'd like to know that, in the event that you were concerned and not gleeful that your niece has been lied to. Again."

The phone ringing startled Carol so much she jumped. She had been who Micah was looking at, and it made him laugh to see her so nervous. Bethany picked up the receiver and said hello, then she got up and handed the handset to her sister.

"You should talk to him. He has plenty to say to you." Carol wouldn't even look at it. "It's Sheppard. I called him just before I came back here to talk to you. But I can see now that there is no talking to you. As usual, you think your way is the only way, and to hell with everything else. I told him you were here and that you were trying to take his daughter from me."

Carol snatched the phone from her, and Micah was startled by the change in her. It was so completely different; from the mean, nasty woman that had been threatening to steal away a child, to someone who looked like butter would not melt in her mouth. She cleared her throat before talking. Micah thought it was to get the rat out of her throat.

"Hello, my darling boy. How are you?" She paused for a moment, and then the room was filled with his voice. Bethany had hit the hands free button on the receiver, apparently. "Well, your grandmother is listening in on us now. She has company too, so I think she's just showing off."

"No, I told her to do that when I called you. I wanted her to hear what I have to say to you. And anyone else that might be there hearing your nasty shit that spewed from your mouth. Just so you know, I've been home since before Christmas. So the money that you want? It's not going to be coming to you because there isn't any. And even if I had a job right now, you were never going to get a thin dime of it." Carol looked around the room, still holding the receiver to her ear. "Did you know that my daughter tells me daily what things you said to her? How I wasn't worth the cum that was spent to make me or Coleen? How I wasn't sending you nearly enough money to take care of a brat like her? You made her cry. And for what? To make you feel better about yourself? Well, since you made it perfectly clear that you wanted her no more than she wanted to be with you, I think that we're done here. You aren't going to—"

"That fucking wife of yours should never have left her with me in the first place. What the hell was I supposed to do with a kid? I haven't the slightest idea what she whined about all the time. She had to have special foods and drinks. Christ, it was like living with my husband, but she was stupider." Sheppard's laughter filled the room. "You think it's funny that she wanted me to cater to her every need? Well, it wasn't. I wish I had never taken her when she needed me."

"Let's get something very clear right now. She never left Mandy with you. You took her." No one said a word when Sheppard made that announcement. "Lisa told me how she'd left Mandy with her own parents, and that you'd wanted her there with you. Argued that it would be better for everyone should you raise her like you had Coleen and me. I even begged Lisa not to leave her with you for an hour, ever. But she got killed a week later and I was grief stricken, along with her parents. That's when you went to Lisa's parents and took my daughter from them. Then you hid her away so that no one could find her, didn't you? But I knew that I'd be home soon, and that I'd take her home with me and we'd be all right."

"Christ, Sheppard, I needed that kid there. Do you have any idea what they were going to do with the money you were sending home? Put it in an account for the child. Christ, had I known about that money beforehand, I might have just gone and gotten her sooner. As it was, it took them almost too long for me to get it. But they sure did make up for it after that. I had a good time while the government was sending it to me. Then it dried up, and not only that, but they took the allotment that I'd gotten already. How fair is that, I ask you? And now I've got things coming due and I'm broke. This is no way to treat me. I practically raised you and your sister when that mother of yours was too drunk to do it on her own. Sheppard, you have to pay me that money. I need it." The line went dead, the dial tone ringing around the room. "I guess he got cut off."

Coleen laughed, and so did Bethany. Micah could see the humor in it as well, but he was watching Carol. She was mad; not just pissed off mad, but he'd bet insane with it too.

Coleen went to the door again and opened it. "It's time you left, Carol. You've very much so overstayed your welcome." Carol stood up and turned to her niece. Micah felt his cat run along his skin, this time in fear for Coleen.

"This isn't over. I demand that you have money sent to me every month, or I'll go to the press." Coleen asked her about what. "I'll make things up to get back at the two of you. You'll regret this if you don't pay me."

"I doubt very much after you leave this house that any of us

105

will think of you again. Maybe if we need a good chuckle, but I'm not sure that even then you'll come to mean much in our lives again." Carol looked as if she were working up something when Coleen grabbed her around the throat. "You spit on me and I will tear your eyes out of your head and piss on them."

Carol was shoved out the door and onto her ass when she missed the step into the doorway. As she laid there screaming at the top of her lungs, Coleen closed the door with a soft click. When she turned to Tony, he stood up and grabbed her before she crumbled. Micah was proud of her in that moment; he'd never even seen her fear until now.

~~~

The restaurant was quiet. Coleen had walked over to Faerie Tales and Dreams with the rest of them when her aunt had finally left. After she was sure that they were safe, Coleen had gone to the restaurant, then the kitchen area, while Grandma told them what had happened. Coleen had invited them over for lunch in an hour. She looked up when she heard someone joining her in the kitchen where she was looking over her notes from the other night. She smiled at Tansy.

"I wasn't sure that anyone would be working here again after Mr. Baker left the other day." Coleen told her that she was going to take the place over. "Oh good. Wow, that's wonderful news. I hated working for him. He was…did you know that he was drunk before he got here in the mornings, and for the most part stayed in his office while we floundered around? I learned more in that few hours you were in charge than I ever did under him. I know that it's rude to talk about someone that has an illness like he does, but I don't think he did us any good

106

while he was here."

"I'm not going to drink on the job. I don't drink at all." Tansy nodded as Coleen pulled one of the larger bowls from the shelf over her head. "Tony and his family are coming over in a few minutes. Would you like to help me whip up something for them?"

"The others are outside. I mean, the under chefs and staff are all here." Coleen told her to get them. "What will we be making? Have you looked in the walk-in? It's full of a lot of food. I wasn't sure what to do with it when it got here earlier. But I've inventoried it all for whoever took over."

Coleen wondered if this place, like their home, was magical, and decided that she wasn't sure she wanted to know. Pulling on a jacket that hung near the offices, she went into the walk-in to see what she could do.

Are you all right? She jumped when Tony spoke to her. *We can communicate now. We have before, but I didn't know if you remembered it. Just think of me when you want to talk and we can on our own link. Are you okay?*

Yes. Tansy and the others are here. We were wondering what you'd like to eat? There is everything we need to make just about anything you want. He told her he'd ask the others. *They're already on their way. I'm sure there is plenty of food here, as I said. I could cook up a nice unhealthy breakfast with all the trimmings.*

Most assuredly yes on the unhealthy part. Do you need help? She asked him for a count and told him she had it covered, but they could set up the tables and chairs. *Got it. There are eighteen counting you. Plus, those in the kitchen with you. They should join us as well.*

All right, twenty-five, give or take. Okay, I'll get started, you finish up out there. And I'll send someone out to set up the buffet table. There is one, right? He laughed and told her there should be one now. *Okay then, I guess that answers my question about this place being the same as our house. The walk-in is full of everything that one might need for a large gathering, and I noticed that it's even larger, with a back area that I have no idea what it might have in it. For now, I'm going to just concentrate on here.* He told her that was probably a good idea.

Nearly an hour later she was taking eggs and omelet fixings to the griddle they'd set up on both ends of the buffet. Tansy was going to be cooking at one end and Matt at the other. She was going to be watching the family to see what they liked and didn't like. She should have known better. They ate all of it. Howie winked at her as he praised just about every item that they had, and especially the breakfast bake.

"Oh my goodness, fresh omelets and fried potatoes. I'm gonna be here every Saturday if this is going on." She glanced at Matt, who had just suggested the same thing not ten minutes ago. "Did you make these biscuits, or do I have someone else to thank for them?"

"Tansy whipped those up. Matt made the breakfast bake, and we all worked on the rest of it." Howie winked at her again. "I also have cinnamon rolls in the oven to come out soon."

The timer went off just as she finished talking about them, and she went to get them out of the oven. She was surprised to see Elroy there. His hat in his hand made her think he was hiding a gun. Thinking of Howie, she wasn't sure what to say to him when he asked her if she was all right and did she need

Anthony

help. Instead of answering him, she let out a long breath and decided to deal with the man.

"If you're hungry, you're welcome to join us. If you've come to cause trouble, I'd not if I were you. I'm not in the mood for your shenanigans today." He just nodded. "Well? What's it going to be? Killed or food?"

"Food. If you don't mind." She told him to grab himself a glass and head to the dining area. When he moved past her, she watched him as she pulled the hot buns from the oven. "I didn't think anyone would be here. I just wanted to tell you... I'm sorry about everything. I fucked up badly, and I'm sorry that you were put in the middle of this. I've not been dealing with things well."

"No you haven't. On a lot of things, I would imagine. And you also owe an apology to those people who looked up to you in the other room. You made them doubt you and themselves, and that's not the way to be a boss." She put the tray on the big butcher block. "Go out there and eat. But if you insult one person out there, I'm going to kick your ass. I've had a really great morning before this, and you'll not fuck it up for me. The Bentleys are out there, and I'm pretty sure I don't have to tell you that they'll hurt you if you mess up again."

"No, you don't have to tell me that. And it would be no less than I deserve." He smiled and moved into the dining area. She saw Howie before she picked up the buns to follow Elroy. He took the pot holders from her and told her to get the other tray. She bent to get it and set it beside the one he'd yet to pick up.

"You're a good woman, Coleen. You could have run him off with a kick to his bottom, but you offered him friendship

109

instead. I don't think I might have been so generous. Thank you for calling out to me when you did. I was ready for him to do something, but you did it all on your own." She told Howie that he would have been very nice to his friend. "No, I don't think so. Not like you were. And you gave him a way to redeem himself to those out there too. That I never would have thought of."

"I was afraid that he had a gun and came back here to kill someone." Howie told her he was armed. "I see. So he was going to shoot us."

"No, he was only going to harm one person, and he's now out there having a fattening breakfast with family who will care for him." Howie picked up the buns and turned. What he'd been talking about hit her hard, that Elroy had planned to kill someone. "Come on now, we're all waiting for these here buns. And you know nobody is gonna get one until I've had one. I'll not have them boys grabbing them all up for themselves."

Breakfast was a success. There were some good natured complaints about how they all were going to need bigger pants, and that there weren't enough buns for everyone to have a fourth helping, but she could see things that the others had not.

The butter was too cold to serve with biscuits, but too hot to use on the sticky buns. The omelets were good, but they didn't have enough burners, nor small pans, to make it work for a crowd any larger than they had now. They'd have to get more fruit in for this sort of thing, and a bigger variety as well. And she'd have to get high chairs too, several the way this family was growing, just for when the family came by. Also, she decided to make the Saturday morning breakfast buffet a family and employee thing, and not open it to the public. This would be for them.

Tony sat beside her as he kissed her on the cheek. "Would you like to help this family grow too?" She wasn't sure what he meant, and then put her hand over her belly. "No, you're not pregnant. You're not in heat either, if that was your next question."

"In heat? I'm just a human, so I don't go into heat. Unless that's a term you always use. Is it?" He told her it was and that she went into heat every month or so, and that he'd be able to smell it. "I see. So when I'm in heat, you can impregnate me and we'll have what? Kittens? Humans? What? And I'm not saying yes to this, just curious about it for right now."

"I understand, and both. Any children we have will be human until they reach a certain age. But since you're not a cat or even a shifter, we might have all human children, or some of both. Would that bother you?" She asked him why he thought it would. "I don't know. I guess I just want to make sure."

"I don't know anything about kids, not really. I didn't even have any interaction with Mandy until recently. Sheppard and I, I guess we sort of shied away from other kids and adults when we were younger." She looked at him. "I guess I should ask you, do you want them? I'm indifferent. Right now anyway. I think I want them, but I would like to wait for a little while. Get my life together and some of this money paid back."

"Joey thinks you've been screwed." She asked him how. "He seems to think they got ahold of a bunch of bills, and since you're paying the firm directly and they're supposedly distributing the money to said bills, they might just be keeping the money for themselves."

"Seriously?" He nodded. "Well, I don't know what to think about that. I mean...it did seem like a really high amount. And to be honest, I was so upset, I never looked at them closely. Do you suppose he can get them reduced? By a lot?"

"He's thinking to get them all to go away. It was fraud on their part, so I'm thinking it's going to be hard for them to prove any of the bills were Micky's. Not to say that there might not have been a few, but they'll have to prove first of all that they're not lying again. And then prove beyond a shadow of a doubt that it was actually him incurring the bills and not someone else. Joey thinks that will be difficult for them to prove after this all comes out." She nodded, seeing where that might be hard to do; once a liar, always a liar, she had always thought. "He is taking Chris out there on Monday to have a little fun and to see the law firm. For him, however, those both could be considered fun. He loves a challenge."

"Then what will happen? I mean, will they have to be more honest in the future? Will this be something that is done just between lawyers and the public might never hear of it? I don't think I'd like that much." He told her that Joey would take them to court if need be, but he had a plan to bring them down. "Down as in out of business?"

"Yes. Men like that, the kind where people trust them to be honest and helpful, they don't deserve to be making money like that." She agreed. "He's also looking into the paperwork to make sure that you weren't divorced in the first place. Joey said there is no reason to believe anything that these people told you."

She thought that might be the best news too. The debt going away would be wonderful, but to not be a widow but a divorcee, she thought that it made her feel better...like she'd had control over ending the relationship between her and Micky. Not that it made much difference in the long run, but she did think it would be great.

Clean up was a mess. Not because there was so much of it to do, but the family insisted on helping. There was a lot of good natured kidding around, and someone had found a radio, so mayhem ensued when they started singing to it...all the wrong words and terribly off key. It was well after noon with they were leaving the restaurant. And Coleen felt better and lighter than she had in a very long time.

"I'm going to go to the store. I don't have a lot of things to wear, and you have to work." He looked so disappointed that she smiled at him. "I don't have a lot of money, so how about I come by — ?"

"Shit." He reached into his pocket and pulled out his wallet. "I meant to give you these yesterday, but you distracted me. Not that I'm complaining...you can distract me whenever you want. But these are for you."

They were credit cards, several of them. All with her name on them, sort of. She wasn't Coleen Bentley. Coleen just looked at them, then at him. This was...very personal to her for some reason.

"They have the wrong name on them." She tried to hand them back to him, but he smiled and dropped to one knee in front of her. Several people stopped to stare. "Get up. What the hell do you think you're doing besides making a fool of yourself? Tony, get up now."

"I love you. Will you marry me? I mean, I could go on and on about how I want to grow old with you, have children and watch them grow up. But you know that, all of it. I do love you. I do want to have as many children as you want whenever you're ready. I'd really love waking up to you for the rest of our days. Which is a very, very long time, in the event I forgot to mention that." She looked around, embarrassed. "Will you say yes before my knee freezes to the sidewalk?"

"Yes, now get up before I have to call your mother and tell her what a dumb ass you are." He did and lifted her up in his arms and swung her around, laughing the entire time. "You're an idiot."

"Perhaps, but I'm your idiot."

The ring was beautiful and she loved it. When he kissed her, pulling her close to him and his warm body, all she could think of was this man loved her. And would forever.

When he told her that he had to go to work, Coleen decided to see if anyone else wanted to go shopping with her. Grandma was all for it, as well as Katie and Gracie. Reggie and the other women said they'd meet her there in an hour. Coleen was giddy and excited. Life, for the first time in a long while, was good.

CHAPTER 8

Sheppard sat in the outer office trying to figure out what he was doing here. On top of being out of work, he had no idea how he was going to afford to put his daughter in preschool should he find a job, and then get a car to get him back and forth to this job. Then there was the added issue of Carol.

He'd never liked her, not even as a child. The few times that his mom had dropped them off with her, usually for a week to a month at a time, she was cruel, heavy handed, and nasty. When he'd found out that she had Mandy, he tried to find out what he could do about having her sent to his grandma. Over a period of about three months all he got was that they were working on it. Or that someone was trying to figure out the circumstances as to why she'd have to leave her aunt's home.

Then out of the blue just before Christmas he was brought into another office much like this one and asked if he needed to get home. He nearly sobbed when they told him what they knew about his home situation.

"Your grandma needs you at home. And I'm to tell you

that she has Mandy as of now." He nodded to his sergeant and asked him how that had come about. "I guess your aunt just put her on a plane one day and said to the staff there that they were to take care of her. No money, no food, and barely enough clothing to survive the cold weather in Ohio. She's a real piece of work, that aunt of yours. By the way, I have already taken care that the money you were sending there has been moved to your grandmother's accounts, and we also took the funds that were allocated for this month back from Ms. Lewis. I have to admit, I didn't have to do that, but after having a long conversation with a few people on your end, it was a great pleasure. I only wish I could have been there when she found out."

"She's going to have a shitfit." Sergeant Williams just smiled. "I petitioned to have the funding stopped weeks ago, and they told me it would take months if not years to complete. Something about proof of guardianship."

"Yes, well, you have very influential friends, as I said. The president called me direct and said that he wanted it done yesterday. And within an hour, it was finished. Also, he said that any man who has his family at home hurting the way that yours is should be able to go and help them in their time of need. He has mustered you out as well."

Before he left he'd been handed a thick envelope that not only had enough cash in it to feed and clothe himself for the next few weeks, but a ticket to get home, as well as information about a car that would pick him up when he landed.

Sheppard had been home on the next flight out, with his money from being let go — very little of it when it was all said and done — in his wallet, and an honorable discharge. Fat lot of good it did him when he couldn't find a job because he was either overqualified for it or had no concrete skills. Not many people wanted a person who could shoot the eye out of a bird at two hundred yards, or dismantle a bomb in the middle of a war zone. He looked up when his name was called.

"Mr. Spencer? My name is Benson Phillips. Thank you so much for coming in on such short notice. Your name came across my desk yesterday, and I thought I'd bring you in and make you an offer of a job." Sheppard was sure he'd misheard. "I have need of a man with your qualifications."

"I don't have any." The man cocked a brow at him. "What I mean is, I have some, but they're not really suited to civilian work. And while I don't really know what I'm doing here, or how my name came to be on your desk, I do appreciate you bringing me here. It's a nice building you have here."

"Did you see any security issues?" Sheppard had a feeling this was a trick question and asked what he meant. "When you got here, you sat in the lobby for a while. Did you see anything that we might improve on in order to keep this building safe, as well as the people who work here? Come to my side of the desk and show me."

He walked around to the other side of the desk and saw that the man had been watching him. Sheppard saw himself looking around, observing as he'd been trained to do for fourteen years. When he asked him what he saw at one point, Sheppard told him.

"Your security staff isn't paying attention to what is going on around them. There is a breach here when they let a man go to the elevators with just a nod. They didn't even look in the pizza box to see if he was carrying anything besides food." Mr. Phillips pointed to another time on the recording. "That man told them that he forgot his badge. No one checked to see if he had been terminated, nor did they check with his department to see if he was able to come up there or not. That's a good way to let a disgruntled employee onto the floor where he worked."

For the next forty minutes Sheppard tore apart the security team. Not just the men and women that worked in that department, but even those that came and went daily that wore a suit and carried briefcases. He even went so far as to point out that most of the time the men and women there were on their cell phones, playing games or texting, another good way to get someone killed. He even criticized the man's lack of security for the garage, where he had parked to come to this meeting.

"No one was at the gatehouse, which was wide open. There was no one there to check to see if I had an appointment, like the other people who came in the front door, or even if I worked there. You're just open for someone to murder you all at your desks." Mr. Phillips asked him about the upper floors. "You don't have any kind of security up here either, where there should be at least some staff. You're here, and unless you have some sort of blocking mechanism on your seat that makes you impervious to bullets, you're a sitting duck."

Sheppard went to sit back down when the man asked him to. "Thankfully, two weeks ago Micah Bentley was here for a meeting that he and I were to have. I don't know if you were aware of this, but he used to be the best homicide cop I ever met, if you don't count his dad, who died too young and left behind a wonderful family. He told me some of what you did just now. He did, however, miss the garage, as well as the food coming up. Micah might have seen it, but he didn't comment."

"I've met him too. Nice family man now. I had no idea he'd been a cop. I knew that his grandfather had been, but that's all." Benson, as he'd asked Sheppard to call him, laughed. "Mr. Bentley the elder, he can talk more than any man I've ever known. But he's a good man, gets to the point eventually, and when he does, you change your mind pretty quick about thinking he's a doddering old fool."

"You are so very right about that. And that he can talk your arm off. My goodness, he can do that. But he's a man who would help you like none other, give you anything you wanted as long as it's not going to hurt his family, and he takes to heart someone that he feels needs something. Like you." Sheppard asked him what he meant. "Yesterday morning Howie came to see me. He didn't need an appointment like anyone else does, just comes in here with a resume that he said he typed up. He tossed it at me and told me I'd be a fool to get killed when there was a brilliant man to help me be safe."

"I don't understand what you mean." Benson just nodded as if he did. "Are you saying that the Bentleys are making you hire me? If so, while I need the job, Benson, I'd rather get it on my own merit. I like myself too much to be beholden to someone that I barely know."

"Two weeks ago, just moments before Micah came to see me, a man got into this building. He killed four people, two of them security, before he made it to my floor and sat where you are now. He held the gun on me for an hour, telling me what I was going to do for him, why I was going to do it, and then he said I was going to die." Sheppard felt a finger of fear on his spine. The man had come as close to death as he'd been, and yet his security was still shit. "Micah told me then that I needed to tighten my security, hire a mercenary type of person, and to fire all the people that worked for me in that department. You see, he had to save my ass. Came in here with his gun blazing and killed my would be murderer."

"He didn't know me then." Benson nodded. "But Howie did this anyway. He told you to hire me because you need to be safe. Why?"

"Why should I hire you or why should I be safe?" Sheppard told him both. "I should hire you because I've looked into your records. Had your CO call me and tell me what sort of person you were. And then not an hour later, I get a call from the president of the United States. Do you know what he said? He congratulated me on hiring a vet, then he told me what the CO couldn't. How long were you out for when you were hurt?"

"Six months." Benson nodded. "We were ambushed. Ten men and myself were set on and holed up for two hours before we got out. We'd been together for a while, so teamwork played a huge factor in us getting out alive."

"That's not the way it really happened, now is it? They survived that day because of you." It wasn't a question, but Sheppard told him it was because of all of them. "No, it was because of you, according to the paperwork I got today. You held the team together, led them out of a bad situation, carrying a man on your back who had been shot. All of this with most of your left leg shot off and a broken arm."

"I did what was required of me." Sheppard felt a tingle of

pain where he'd been hurt. "Any one of us would have done the same thing. It's what we're trained for."

"Does your family know? Do they have any idea what really happened over there?" He told him they did not, and he would like to keep it that way. "All right. But I want you to come here and keep my family safe. And that's what most of them are to me. Ninety percent of the people working for me at my first business are here with me now. I don't want to have to ever make another phone call like I had to that day. And if I have to, I want to be able to say with a true heart that I did everything within my power to make it so that they'd not be hurt."

"I'm not saying I'll do it, but you'd be all right with me going in and taking over? No questions asked about how I get the place under control?" Benson told him so long as he did it legally, he just wanted it done. "I carry a gun. I think they all should."

"I agree." Sheppard waited for the catch. There was nearly always a catch when someone gave you full control. "I don't want to have to worry every time that door opens that someone is going to kill me. I want to be able to go home at night to my wife and children. I want to be able to go to work and think about my job and what I do, and not about the gunman that could be lurking in the halls. So long as you do it legally, as I said, and you apprise me of what you're doing, you can take control of the security here."

"And the pay?" The man slid a folder over to him and Sheppard picked it up. He was nervous that it was going to be less than he needed, because as much as he wanted this to work—because he loved the idea that Benson was telling him about—he needed money coming in. And insurance. But the offer was almost double what he'd hoped for. He looked at Benson. "This is a lot of money."

"It is. As far as I'm concerned, it's not enough if I can feel good about this place. And you'll also have insurance, paid by the company, and a car to use as you see fit. If you need to upgrade the security cameras or anything else, just let me know and I'll have it done. Oh, and as of the moment you walked in the door downstairs, you were a part of this company. I'd be an idiot not to have you here. All that, including the other perks you'll have, start today, right now."

Benson stood up and put out his hand. Sheppard took it and felt...well, he felt pretty fucking wonderful. As they worked out when he'd begin the firings, as well as the revamping of the systems, Sheppard had to keep telling himself this was real and that he owed Howie Bentley a great deal.

~~~

The offices were coming along nicely. Tony had wanted to have it open by summer, but at the rate things were going, it might be sooner than that. He was just moving to one of the other rooms when he heard someone talking just around the corner. He moved to see what it was, and saw a little boy with a tear stained face talking to one of the workers.

"You have to save him. He's all I have in the entire world." Tony moved forward to see that the little boy was holding a small dog in his arms, and it looked to have been hit by a car. Tony moved to be level with the little guy and looked into the dog's pain filled eyes.

"What happened to him?" The little boy said nothing, and Tony looked at him. "Do you know what happened to him and you're not telling me, or you don't know?"

"He was hurt really bad." Tony asked him by who. "I don't know, but my stepfather, he don't like dogs, and I tried really hard to keep him away from the man next door, but he was needing me to protect him. The poor thing is hurt real bad. Can you help him please?"

Tony wasn't sure who needed the protecting, nor who was hurting who. The boy was jumping around too much for him to keep up. But one thing was clear, the dog was hurt and needed attention.

"Did he hit you too?" The little boy again said nothing, but Tony knew what he was thinking. Taking the dog from him carefully, he moved down to the room that he knew had been set up for work. "I'm going to examine him first. Do you want to stay? He's going to be very upset."

"Yes, he's a good dog but don't deserve this." When Tony nodded, he pulled on some gloves to protect his hands in case the dog decided to bite when he hurt. "My name is Marshall Finley. The dog's name is Donk. It's a dumb name, but my little sister called him that before she and Mom got killed."

"Was this long ago?" He said about last year. "And you live with your stepfather then. I guess some people don't like dogs as much as you and I do."

"No, he hates about everything. Including me when I'm stupid. I try really hard, but I can't do some of the things he wants me to." Marshall watched Tony's every move. When he figured out what was wrong with the dog, he turned to him.

Marshall started to cry. "I just know you're going to tell me he ain't worth saving. But I wish you would try real hard. I don't have much money, but I can work here if you want. I can sweep up and stuff."

"I'm going to give him something for the pain, then I'm going to set his leg and wrap his ribs up. He'll be just fine so long as he gets proper care, and I'm going to make sure that he gets it." Marshall threw himself at him and hugged him tightly. As he was holding the little boy, his grandma came to the doorway. "This is my grandma. She was going to take me to lunch, but I'm going to be busy for a bit. Do you think you could do me a huge favor and escort her for me?"

"I don't have no money to take a pretty lady out to lunch, but I'll make sure she's all right." He looked at his grandma then back at him before Marshall continued. "Are you sure you don't wanna take her? She's really pretty and all."

"Well thank you, young man. And there will be the two of us...my Gracie is going too, Tony's mom." Marshall nodded. "And since I invited him to lunch, I'm paying. And it would be a pleasure to have you come and eat with us while Tony works on your lovely animal. I've known him all his life, and I know that he'll take very good care of your poor puppy."

After he left, his mom contacted him through their link. *This poor young man is beside himself with nervousness. He's worried to death that he'll embarrass us two pretty women. I love this kid. Can you tell me what's going on and why we're having lunch again when we've just left the diner?*

Tony told her what he'd told him. *I don't know who his stepfather is, do you? I mean, he just told me his name but nothing more. I don't suppose he's mentioned anything to you.*

Yes. His momma died some months ago, taking his little sister with her. A car crash that happened in another state when she'd been visiting her mother. I don't know this boy's stepfather, but I'd say he needs a lesson in rearing children. Marshall has a heck of a bruise on his back and both his arms. And he needs a good meal or two. She laughed. *Reggie is looking into this now. She came by to pick up something to take to Micah and saw us. I don't think I'd want to be the stepfather right now.*

No, me either.

When Donk was asleep, Tony set his leg, but didn't cast it, then took him to x-ray. He wanted to make sure that he'd not missed anything in his exam, and found that poor Donk needed a few good meals himself. And that someone had been hurting the dog for a while now. He had some scarring on a couple more ribs besides the one that was broken, and his body had a few bruises. He told his mom what he'd found and asked her to tell Reggie.

I'm pretty sure that when I tell Reggie she might go and get her gun. That girl can resort to violence quicker than anyone I know. Most of the time it's with good reason, but she frightens me just a little. Tony laughed as he worked on the dog. *This little boy, do you suppose he's being abused to where someone has to step in? You know how much abuse to children, no matter the age, angers me.*

Yes, I know Mom, but I don't know. Other than the hug, that's all I got from him. When I asked him about how his dog got hurt, he explained how his stepfather doesn't like much of anything, including him. When he was finished wrapping the dog's ribs and had a cast on his leg, Tony put him in one of the new cages so he could rest. He told his mom what was going on with him.

I'll tell him. He'll be so relieved, I think. When I bring him back there, I would very much like for you to set him to watch over the dog. I don't think he should be going home until we have a look or two, do you? He told her it would be okay with him to have the little boy hanging around for a bit longer. *Of that I have no doubt. Oh, and I just went by the restaurant a few minutes ago, and it looks like Coleen is getting a nice delivery. Did she agree to take the restaurant from your grandda?*

She did. I don't think she's very confident in her abilities in running it, but she said she'll give it a try. Also, I guess that Pip is supposed to close down early tonight to reset Faerie Tales and Dreams for Valentine's Day. The faeries are excited to get it ready. When I was in there earlier this week, I could see some of the things they were working on. I might have to go there for something for Coleen. Tony remembered that he needed to get the other women in his life something too. *When are Grandma and Grandda leaving?*

In two weeks. I think they're very excited about that, too. You guys got them the most perfect gift in that cruise. I swear to you that's all she's talked about. And my trip with all of you this summer is the best gift you could have gotten me. I'm looking forward to that as much, if not more. He was really glad now that Pip had suggested the trips. *I just heard from Reggie. Things are not what they seem, it appears. The young stepfather has been looking for the boy since this morning. Apparently he's become quite a problem for everyone, including the school and the neighbor. And Mr. Finley didn't hit the boy. Apparently he was injured stealing the neighbor's dog. Again.*

Like how? She told him how the boy had done it in the past. *He crawled under the fence to get him? Do you know why he'd do...*

please tell me that there is a good reason for this. And that he'd not let the dog get away and get hit by a car.

Yes, there was a good reason, darling. Apparently he thinks that the neighbors are abusing their animals. Which I can guess that they are. And young Marshall here has been trying to get someone to notice for months now. Much to the dismay of not just the neighbors, but his stepfather as well. He's not beaten the boy as we thought. The next-door neighbor throws things at the youngster, and Sherman, his stepfather, has gone to the station about it, but of course nothing was done until now. Marshall is something of a hero, I think. He asked about the mom and sister. *Yes, I'm afraid that's true. His stepfather is grieving very badly, and has now admitted that he might have been somewhat short to his son — not stepson, but son — but has never hit him.*

He supposed that he had jumped to conclusions on what he thought was going on and had colored things for his mom. He told her he was sorry. She laughed at him.

Darling, I would rather you jump to those sort of conclusions than to be indifferent to what goes on around you. All you did was talk to me, you didn't accuse anyone. And Reggie is coming to the restaurant where we're at to get young Marshall. She's with his father. The poor man is so upset, she said.

I bet he is. Tony checked on the pup once more. *But this little dog has been abused badly. And not just recently either. I think we need to do something about that as well.*

Done. He was almost afraid to ask her. When she laughed, he was positive that he hadn't. *Reggie and Mr. Finley have gone to see the neighbor, she told me. I'm thinking that the pup will be going home with Marshall when he's better, and not the monster that hurt him. And before you ask, yes, Reggie was very nice. For her anyway.*

Tony spent the next two hours watching over his first patient in his new offices. It was really too big for what he wanted to start with, but he'd also set up two rooms in the back that were furnished so that if an animal had to stay for a longer period of time, the family could stay with it. He had found over the years that having someone that was familiar to them made the animals heal much faster. And stay calmer, which helped everyone. He supposed the same could be said for people as well.

"Okay, you have to explain something to me." Tony laughed when he answered the phone a bit later and it was a very frazzled sounding Coleen. "This place has magic like our house. So...okay, I don't really understand it, but that's not why I called. How do I know what it is going to order for me, in the way of food, and what it won't? I mean, as of right now, I have about seven hundred pounds of garlic cloves."

He laughed, he just couldn't help it. "It can't order what there are many varieties of. Such as, if you think you need flour? The magic won't know if you mean flower as in the blossoms or flour that you bake with. And even if you were to say baking flour, it wouldn't know which one to get for you. There are too many variations on it. Rye, wheat, and so on." She said okay. "Bacon might be tricky too, Micah told me. Such as peppered bacon, which he loves, is there all the time at his house, but Reggie prefers just bacon. That comes in too, but in much smaller quantities, as she doesn't eat it as much as he does. He said it took him a few days to think about peppered bacon and not pepper on bacon. He had a sack of peppercorns on several pounds of bacon, and that wasn't what he wanted. Or so he said."

"So should I need tea for drinking and for using to cook with, I more than likely would have to order that. As well as coffee for the restaurant, right?" He told her that was right. "This is very complicated; you know that? I have to think about everything I want, and even then I barely get it right. It's driving me crazy."

"You could have it not do any of it at all for you. Simply tell one of the faeries there that is the way you wish it and it'll happen." She said she thought that she'd like for the magic to be there, but she'd have to get used to it. "Then have it only order, say, fish for the day, beef, or chicken. Veggies could be a standing order, and you could have it make a certain brand of coffee and tea. You'd have to be specific."

"I can work that." She sighed heavily. "I don't know if we'll be ready by next week. The staff is still trying to figure out how to take an order in a restaurant this size, as well as I'm having a little issue with the plumbing. Not major, but our water pressure seems to be up and down. The dishwasher can't wash well if there is no pressure."

"That is out of my realm of helping you. But I can call the water department and have them look for you." She told him she'd done that and they were coming out at four. "So you'll be late?"

"No. I don't think so. Matt has said he'd stay and wait for them if I had to go. Did you know that he is a wolf?" He said that he did. "I guess you guys sort of sniff asses and figure that out."

"Nothing so nasty, but we can sense one another. If you'd like, I can make it so you can sense it as well." She asked him what he meant. "I could convert you. Not now, not with all the stuff you have going on, but when you want. You'd be down for a few days resting, but I would love to have you as a cat as well."

"And I'd get the whole healing thing too." She sounded almost too eager about that part, and he asked her about it. "I burned myself today. No biggie, but it hurts like a mother fucker right now. I do that sometimes. Think that I can simply be flame retardant, and blister up like I'm set in oil."

"I can heal you." She was quiet and he wondered about that until he heard the voice near her. Someone wanted to know about flowers on the table. "If they're not from Faerie Tales and Dreams, I'd tell them you have it covered. If you don't mind using family."

"The arrangements have been made for the tables and entrance, thanks. But should I have a need in the future, I'll give you a call." When the person thanked her, he heard the door shut. "This is the fourth person that has come by to ask me for some sort of help. First it was the linen guy. I had to nearly throw him from the place when he just had to taste what we were making. Believe it or not it was just soup to help out over at the shelter. We had lots of veggies and.... Never mind. You get the picture. Then later this woman showed up to tell me she had the best coffee in the world. Yuck. And then not an hour after that, someone came in wanting to print my menus. I explained that we had a computer that did it just fine, and I thought she was going to have a heart attack. What a pretentious bitch."

"They know that you're going to be huge and want to be a part of it. They want to ride on your coattails, so to speak." She snorted. "You are, love. This will be just the beginning for you. Everyone knows it but you."

"I want it to be the end." He laughed. "Okay, I'll come by later to have you look at this burn. Unless you want to come by and taste test some chicken dishes. And expect a lot of garlic."

He was still laughing when Marshall and his dad showed up to have a talk with him. Mr. Finley was a very nice man, but hurting.

CHAPTER 9

"I'm here to pick up my grandniece, Amanda Spencer. My name is Carol Lewis." The woman stared at her and Carol wanted to slap the piss out of her. But she smiled her best smile and repeated her earlier story. "Her grandma told me to come by and get her so that we could spend the day together before I left for home. I won't be able to see her so often now. She lived with me for a little while."

"Your name isn't on the list, I'm afraid. We have a list of pick up names that we establish at the beginning of the school year. That way no one can come by and pick up someone that they're not supposed to. You can understand that. You'd not want anyone to come for your grandniece that's not supposed to, would you?" Carol wanted to stomp her foot. "I'm very sorry, but without a note from someone in her family, or at least a call, there isn't any way for me to release her to you. You'll have to make arrangements to have that to take her."

"But this was spur of the moment. Just go on and get her, and she and I will have a very lovely afternoon." The woman just stared at her without moving, and Carol felt her temper heat up. "It would be nice if you did it sometime today while I'm still young enough to enjoy her. Get a move on, I don't have all day."

She'd had tone, Carol knew it, but smiled to hide it. Damned people. Why were there so many rules to get a fucking child out of school nowadays? In her day you wanted your kid, you just went and got them. Now they had rules and notes to be passed around. When the woman moved back into her cubbyhole of an office, Carol thought of what she was about to do.

Take the girl to the hotel and demand that they pay her for her trouble. It wasn't kidnapping. She wasn't demanding a ransom or anything. She just wanted to get paid for all the suffering she'd had from keeping the kid at her house. In retrospect she more than likely should never have gone to get her in the first place. But it had seemed like a good way to get some extra welfare that she'd read some of the lower level people were doing. Have a bunch of kids to get lots of money to spend on soft drinks and steaks and shit. The money coming from the army had been a real plus she'd not counted on. But damn, oh damn, it had come in handy.

The kid's grandparents had only just found out that hour that their little girl had been killed. Mandy's grandparents, she amended in her head. It had been a piece of cake for her to tell them that she'd take the child for the day, and let them deal with things. It wasn't as if they didn't know her; her nephew was married to their kid, for Christ's sake. So take her she did. And went straight to the welfare office to apply for some help. It had taken her nearly an hour to get them to see she was going to need it, when all the kid had done was whine the whole time about being hungry.

Carol supposed she might have given the grandparents the correct information about where she'd been staying, or even better, a working phone number. But the added six hundred dollars a month to raise the kid up would make anyone take precautions. Then there was the check that was direct deposited into her account with Sheppard's name on it. And after the first month, with the extra money coming in regular like, Carol decided to try her best to double down her money. That had been a mistake, she knew that now.

Gambling had never been something she was good at. She seldom won anything, and even when she did it wasn't as much as she spent. Then the week that she'd brought the kid to her house, she'd won over six grand. Just like that, she knew the kid was going to improve things. But there had never been a pay off like that again, not even a six dollar one.

As the days turned into weeks, then months, she grew not just to hate the kid but everything about her. The way she talked all the fucking time. She had to have clean clothing, and she had no idea how to shower herself and get her hair washed. Carol was never so glad to get rid of something in her entire life as she was that brat. Then the money was gone.

Not only was there no more checks coming in, but the money that had been put in her account for the month was taken from her too. Then when she'd tried to use her welfare money, there was some kind of note on it telling her to call the office. Fuck that shit, she wasn't going to go down there and tell them anything. But that money was gone now too. She wasn't even getting what she had been before the kid. Zip. Nothing. Zero.

It was the only reason she'd kept her until the end of the month, to make sure that if anyone came by to see if she was there, the brat would be. That just wasn't right. She figured that eventually someone would know that she didn't have the kid and stop the money. Carol had figured the way the government worked, it might be a few years. But not only had it been nearly the same week, but Carol was pretty sure that it had been within hours after calling her sister to tell her to be at the airport to get the kid.

"No way was she able to get the results that fast." Carol looked at the three kids coming down the hallway toward her. They weren't her grandniece, but she didn't like them any better. Lunging at them like she was going to attack had them jumping back and Carol laughing. Kids were so fucking stupid. She heard someone clear their throat, and she looked at someone else from the cubbyhole in the back. If she had to start this shit over, she was going to hurt someone for it. Christ, was everyone in this state stupid?

"Ms. Lewis, you really should be going. As we have said, there is no way we're giving you Mandy. You can wait at her house if you want, or you can bring in a note from her grandmother tomorrow so we have time to verify things. We aren't able to just give a child to anyone that comes for them." Carol asked her why not. "It's for the safety of the children. We take a great deal of pride in the fact that we've never had any trouble with our children going home with the wrong person or persons."

"But I'm her great aunt. Bring her out here and let me see her. She'll tell you who I am and that I practically raised her after her momma died." Not true, but how were these idiots to know? "Mandy is my only grandniece, and I just want to spend some time with her. Is that too much to ask? You people are making it very hard on an old woman who just wants to spend time with the kid...with Mandy."

"If it were true, then that would be fine. But we both know that every word out of your mouth is a lie." She turned and looked at the man coming toward her. He looked familiar, but she just couldn't place him. "It's Sheppard, Carol. Mandy's father. And I do not appreciate you making the school call me away from work to come down here and tell you to stay away from my daughter. I thought this was cleared up the other day when I told you to keep away from her."

"Sheppard?" This man was bigger than she remembered. And he was dressed in a very nice suit and tie. She didn't know a lot of things, but she did know expensive. "What bank did you rob to get yourself all gussied up like this? And no, the matter is not closed until I say it is. You should be giving me money, not spending it on fancy suits that make you look ridiculous."

When he moved — not aggressively, no, but enough that she could see that he was armed — Carol took a step back from him. And the hostler at his side looked like something out of all the gangster movies that she'd ever watched. When he handed the lady at the desk something, Carol wanted to scream that he was going to shoot them all, but all he did was open his coat jacket up and show the woman at the desk that he was carrying a gun. She supposed that he was something important to them.

137

Well, he wasn't to her, only in that he should be giving her cash to keep away and not threats.

"What are you doing here? I thought you were moving away to some other state to get a job?" He only glared at her, then turned to the woman that had more than likely called him.

"I'd like you to make note that if this woman comes here again to get my child, you should call the police. Or even if you see her hanging around the school. She's not a nice person. And has more than likely decided to kidnap Mandy for some reason. I'd like her not to ever be around her." Carol slapped him on the back. Sheppard turned to her. "I'm not that little boy anymore, and you'd do well to remember that. I will not tolerate you touching me in any way, even if you feel the sudden urge to hug me. I will snap you in half without a second thought."

"Fuck you. You owe me for watching her while you were playing war in that foreign country. The people that you worked for, they took what was mine and I need it. I was living very well until you had them take money from my personal account." He only crossed his arms over his chest and she took a step back from him. Sheppard had grown up, and she was a little afraid of him. "You look like you can afford to hand over a few hundred dollars. It's the least you can do for me taking care of her while you were gone. Then maybe I'll go away and not bother you again. Unless I run a little short. You owe me, Sheppard. You and that bitch of a sister of yours."

"I'm not giving you anything, Carol. Nor will Coleen. She's happy now, and so am I. Just crawl back into your hole and leave us all alone. And if I were you, once I got to my little place in hell, I'd stay there rather than risk getting hurt. By me."

The lady at the desk laughed. "Now, we're done here. You are not getting my child ever again, and I am not giving you any money. As a matter of fact, I'd like it very much if you were to never see any of us again for any reason, and that includes Grandma. Stay out of her life too."

"What a way to talk to me. I'm your aunt, not some woman you met on the street and took home with you. And you'll not be calling me by my given name again, either. Don't you dare disrespect me like that. If you think you're just showing off, I'll show you a thing or two." He turned and walked away from her. "Come back here, you little fucker. I'm not finished talking to you yet."

"Miss Lewis, I'm going to have to ask you to lower your voice and to stop using such language. We're a school with children present. They should not be subjected to such words here at a learning institution." Carol just stared at her. Did she not just see what had happened? "And I've called the police as Mr. Spencer asked me to when I called him. You'll have to leave or the police will arrest you."

"You mother fucking, cunt sucking shit hole." When the shocked look on her face was replaced with anger, Carol stepped closer to her. "You are nothing but a white trash, fucking bitch who more than likely eats pussy for lunch. How dare you call the police on me? I told you that I'm her great aunt and that I only wanted to spend the day with her. You're the one that got all pissy and decided to call Sheppard here. Where was he anyway? Working for some fucking mobster? That would be something he'd do. Fuckers, all of you."

When she too turned her back on her, Carol saw red. Did

no one respect one another anymore? She was just trying to get herself some money, and everyone was treating her like she'd killed someone. Fuck this shit. She turned and left the school just as the police were pulling up. When one of them asked her to come along with them, Carol spit on him. It was out of her mouth and on his face before she could think that it might not be such a good idea to do that to a man of the law.

She was on the ground with her face in the dirt before she could tell him that she'd not meant to hit him with it. Of course, she had, but he didn't have to know that. Instead of being able to defend her actions, like blaming it on the people who had pissed her off, she was tossed into the back of a cruiser so fast that she'd barely gotten her purse gathered up. Then the cop, who had just a little spittle on his chin, reached in beside her and took her handbag.

"Give that back to me right this minute. I will not have you going through my things like I've done something terrible. Wipe your face off and grow some balls, you fool; it's not like I pissed on you. If you want, I have some stored up for you. But you just need to give me a minute to knock your ass to the ground and drain my bladder on you. You cock sucker." He slammed the door in her face. "Mother fuckers. What is wrong with you people?"

When someone got into the front of the cruiser, she tried to reason with him. He just told her to shut up and then adjusted the mirror over the dash so that she could see herself. Fucker was more than likely recording shit too. But as far as she could see she'd done not one thing to warrant them treating her like this.

"It was just a little spit. I do it all the time when I'm pissed off." He said nothing as he started the car. "It's not like I got anything you can catch. I'm a good Christian woman. I don't go to church or shit like that, but I do know that God looks down over me."

"I'm sure He does."

Carol could hear just a little sarcasm there, but decided to ignore it. When they pulled in front of the stationhouse a few minutes later, she saw her sister standing there with Sheppard. There was the bitch that had caused it all. Almost as soon as she was cleared of the car, she tried to go and tear her face off. When she was jerked back, she started to spit again when the man drew his gun. She looked at Bethany when it was apparent that he wasn't going to back down.

"What the fuck did you do that for? Call them up and tell them to take my money? I need it, damn it. I was only going to take the kid for a bit and have you pay me to get her back, but you had to just get all shitty about it." Bethany told her that was kidnapping. "No, it's not. Christ, you are forever making something out of nothing. I was only going to take her for a little while, not kill her or anything. I just want what is coming to me. And I don't think some cash is too much to ask for."

"That's kidnapping. Taking someone without permission is kidnapping." She asked the stranger who she was. "Chris Bentley, the attorney for Mr. Spencer and his daughter. We're pressing charges, Officer."

"No you're not. Sheppard, I swear to Christ, you are as stupid as your mother was. How the fuck can you even think this shit...? Oh, I see. Trying to impress this bitch, are you? Well back the fuck off and tell them to leave me alone. Just go to the fucking bank and get me money. I don't care if you have to rob it. I want my fucking money returned to me now." She looked at Chris. "Honey, you're barking up the wrong tree with him. He doesn't have a pot to piss in, and him trying to get into your pants? Well, you'd be better off trying to fuck this cop here."

"Take her please, before I hurt her." Carol was still screaming at the woman when she was dragged away. These fuckers were going to pay for treating her this way.

~~~

Coleen stood in the walk-in and looked at all the food without really seeing it. She had a lot of it, that was about all that registered, but what it was, she didn't have a clue. All she could think about was her aunt and what she'd tried to do with little Mandy.

When the door opened behind her all she did was turn to see who it was. Matt and Tansy had become good friends over the last several days, and she was sure that they were going to be very helpful when the restaurant opened tomorrow night.

"I was thinking that we'd make a nice vegetable soup with some homemade gnocchi. And french bread with basil crust to go with it." She watched as Matt began gathering up some of the fresh things on the long table in the middle of the fridge. "We have to come up with a poultry entrée, as well as a beef one. Tony suggested some kind of steak, but I thought you two could decide what it would be."

"How about a garlic rosemary Cornish hen with fresh grilled green beans? A starch of boiled potatoes in a light butter sauce. That way if we have any leftover, we can make a nice chicken pot pie for the next night as a side dish. Serve it up in small pots." Coleen told Tansy that she loved that idea, and to get the hens ready. "If you don't mind, I'll fix one up now and we can sort of test drive it. I heard that Howie is coming over later anyway."

"Yes, my man of the hour." When she got out three of the hens that she was sure weren't there before, she looked over at Matt. He didn't look so confident; or maybe it was something about beef he didn't care for. "Matt? Do you have any ideas?"

"About five years ago I was filling in as a dishwasher in one of the bigger restaurants in Chicago. It wasn't like this; what I mean is, it was an old place, and you sort of had to make do with what they had. Anyway, I heard the head chef say that beef was sort of a boring meat. There are only so many things you can do with it — grill, bake, or even roast it — but all of it is just that, beef." She asked him what he had in mind. He looked around before turning to her. "Not beef. How about I make something like an herb roasted pork tenderloin in individual portions that has a peach glaze over it? Then grilled peaches to accompany it, along with the grilled green beans that Tansy suggested."

"And the fish entrée? What would you do? I have trout, and we can get in some salmon too." He nodded and she laughed. "I don't think I'm up for both."

"No, sorry. The trout. To me that just says class for some reason. And just grilled without the head this first time, and some grilled roasted carrots alongside of it. I don't know why, but green beans just don't go with fish for me." She nodded. "Do you want to test drive all of this as well?"

Test drive. She'd first heard it used by Howie, and since

he'd been coming around daily to test things, all the staff, including the dishwashers, were using it. It had a nice ring to it, and she loved the man for it. She loved all the Bentleys now.

"Yes, we might as well. We want things to go well tomorrow night, and I'd really like to know beforehand how long something takes to fix. I have an idea, but I don't want people pissy for our first opening." He nodded and she stopped him. "Bread will be coming from the diner. The cook there has some things that he wants to try, and he said that the men there won't appreciate it as much as we might."

When he left her, she moved to the back of the room. It was huge, bigger than most larger restaurants she'd ever worked in. And it was well stocked. As she made her way to one of the long shelves, Coleen counted the trout there and smiled. She guessed that three for tonight would be enough. Might as well have the family over again. Just as she reached for Tony to ask him if he wanted them to come over, the door opened again and there stood Micah.

"What is it?" He just shook his head and smiled at her. "I don't know if you are aware of this or not, but you're not very comforting when you do that. There is something very scary about a big man showing off all his sharp teeth. And since I know what you are and why your teeth are so sharp, it scares me even more. What are you doing here?"

"I'm trying to be charming." She told him he'd failed. "Oh well. I have a favor to ask you. And it's okay if you say no."

"I know that." He nodded and opened the door again. "So not in here, I take it. And why not, may I ask? Do you need a witness in the event that I hurt you? I can you know; I'm not

144

your mate or in love with you. I'm not even sure that I like you all that much."

"You can't hurt me because I'm your leader. And if you did, Reggie might hurt you. We both know that she's by far meaner than both of us together. You may not want to do this favor for me. So in answer to your question, my favor to you is not to fucking freak out...not my words, but there you have it." She stared at him, then at the door. "Please?"

"No. I don't know why, but I don't think I want to go out there with you. I've had a pretty good day today—not fantastic, but not too bad either—and I just know that going out there is going to really mess it up." He promised her it wouldn't. "Now see, you just told me not to freak the fuck out. I'm pretty sure that's not something you say to someone that you're trying to get to do what you want."

"What if I told you that Tony sent me in here to get you?" She asked him if he had. "Yes. I won't lie to you. But in this, I won't tell you why either. It's not the way it's done."

"Done? As in, I don't know, how you kill someone off? Or are you planning something else? Like you're going to chop me up in little pieces and serve me to your pack." He just shook his head at her, laughing. "It's not funny."

"No, it is. And its leap, not pack. I'm a cat, not a wolf." She glared at him. "You're funny when you try to be all macho like."

"I don't like you." He laughed harder. "I don't want to be hurt, Micah. Can you promise me that I won't be hurt if I go out there with you? Like I said, I've had a pretty good day, and being hurt again today would just suck big balls."

"I promise you with all my heart that you won't be hurt if you come out of this icebox and go into your kitchen. I swear to you on my life that no one will ever harm you so long as I'm alive, too. You're my family now, and I know that you do like me, maybe even love me a little, but I won't let anyone harm you. I promise you." She knew then that what he was saying was as solid as the floor she was standing on. "Will you join me in the kitchen?"

"Yes. But if this turns to shit, I'm going to make sure you don't have your favorite cake on your birthday, and you won't get another sticky bun from me." He told her it was a deal. She moved to the door. "You'd better be right. I'll tell Reggie if you're not."

"She's here too." Coleen nearly stopped moving, but he was behind her now and he gave her a small shove to get her out of the walk-in and into her kitchen. The entire family was there, and she felt her eyes fill when they all yelled happy birthday to her. She looked at Tony when he pulled her into his arms.

"We didn't think you'd be in there long enough for us to get this set up. Then we weren't sure you were ever going to come out." He kissed her. "Happy birthday, my love."

"I don't know how you found out." She looked at her brother, who was wearing the stupidest paper hat she'd ever seen. "Ah, I should have known. You were always telling people when to get you birthday gifts."

"If I had waited for you, we would never have gotten a thing." He kissed her on the forehead. "Happy birthday, little sister. I'm glad that I was home for this."

"Me too." She leaned on his chest and then hugged him.

"Me too. This is very nice; don't you think?"

"It is. Here, I got you something." She took the gift but laid it on the table by the big cake. She'd bet anything that Matt or Tansy had made it, probably even both of them. After she ran to her office, she picked up the gift she'd gotten for her brother just that morning and took it out to him. "You remembered my birthday? How nice of you. I thought about marking it on your calendar, but figured you of all people would remember my birthday." Coleen called him an idiot and laughed

Her grandma was there, as well as Mandy and some of the family that she'd yet to meet; Alta Cole, grandmother to Rylee; Barron and his daughter and her son; Chris's dad, Allen Black, as well as a few hundred faeries. Even Shane and Walter were there, both of them getting better all the time from nearly being killed a few months ago. It was the first time in a very long time that there had been any kind of celebration for either her or her brother. She was glad that it was with this family more than anyone else she could think of.

As they moved things out into the dining area, she smiled at the decorations that had been put up. The faeries had become as much a part of her life as Tony had. They had gone well beyond anything that she'd ever dreamed of to make the restaurant look festive. In addition to the flowers, and there were hundreds of those, there were ribbons and candles, all bright with magic. And there were brightly colored lights. Their magic was beautiful even where they sat waiting on her. Their wings, beautifully displayed in the upper darkness of the ceiling, made it look like the Fourth of July with all the fireworks going off.

Sheppard loved the vest she'd gotten him. Reggie had helped her get it. She'd called in a few favors and had had the bulletproof vest not just shipped here overnight for her, but had made sure that Sheppard's name was on it, as well as the new company that he worked for. Phillips Banking was lucky to have Sheppard working for them.

The gifts were opened with a lot of fanfare. Someone even remembered to get something for the younger ones. The baby, young Michael, who Micah and Reggie were adopting, was too young, but the little girls loved the dolls. Mandy had gotten a smaller version of the vest her dad had gotten, without all the bells and whistles. Coleen had a feeling that she was going to be just like her dad in all ways, and wanted her to be aware of all the safety things from the beginning.

Howie and Katie gave her the deed to the building and the restaurant. Micah and Reggie gave her several old cookbooks that she adored. The others gave her cooking things, and a set of her very own knives…better than the ones that she'd had to sell in Vegas. She got a camera that she'd been wanting, as well as everything to set up a dark room. And so many other very nice gifts. But it was the one from Tony that she loved the most. He'd gotten her a honeymoon package that would take her to every five-star restaurant around the world. She had never been so happy as she was right now.

"So, was it worth coming out of the icebox for?" She hugged Micah to her. "I have one more thing for you. It's not a lot, but you'll like it. I've okayed for Tony to convert you into a panther like us."

"He needs your permission?" He told her that he did; he

didn't usually make a big deal out of it, but Tony had wanted it to be official. "I want it now, but he said we had to wait. I can see where he has a point, but I hate having to go see him every time I burn myself or a knife slips, which happens a lot. Not that it happens nearly as much as it used to, but it is annoying."

"You know, you can pretty much control that. Him changing you, I mean." She asked him how. "Well, when he's his cat, you can command him, sort of, to convert you. He'll do it because he loves you as well. But when he gets it in his head to do it, even if someone suggests it, Tony won't be able to stop him. There have been times, I've heard, that the cat in us is much stronger than the human part. I think Tony's panther would like to see you changed as much as you would."

When he winked at her and walked away, she knew what she had to do. After the opening tomorrow, they were going to be closed up for a few days anyway, to regroup. She'd get him to do it then. Coleen was going to be a cat by this time next week or know the reason for it. Maybe she'd even practice her skills as a big panther and eat her aunt just for being a bitch. Then she thought of being sick. Her aunt would not go down well.

CHAPTER 10

Joey loved Vegas, especially seeing it through Chris's eyes. She'd been here before, of course; having had a client here for a while and had visited them. But she'd never actually been on the strip. As they walked the crowded streets and visited the many shops, he kept a close eye on her and her reactions. As they entered the next chocolate store, he decided to call the car and have them come and get some of their purchases. He was glad that they'd taken the jet out here, or they might have had to ship some of it home.

When his phone rang, he stepped onto the sidewalk to answer. It wasn't any quieter, but he wasn't crowded into a corner with a dozen or so people who could listen in on his conversations. As soon as he saw who it was, he had to smile. Reggie could work miracles.

"Okay, you owe me. One of the Supreme Court judges is going to meet you at the firm in the morning. He hasn't had any contact with the firm personally, so he said he can do as you ask and be just a witness until things get hinky. He's a tiger, by the way. Did you know that they're called leaps too? Anyway, he's going to meet you two there, and he wants to know if you can send him what you have. I suggested that he be as surprised as the others, but he told me to ask you." Joey said he'd send it over. "I figured you'd say that. Oh, and I'm supposed to ask you to get one of those huge-assed candy bars for Howie. He wants to give it to Katie." He told her they were there now and asked what flavor. She told him. "I guess that's her favorite. To be honest, I've never seen her eat chocolate, so I was kind of concerned that Howie wanted it—it would be like him—but Micah said that she really does love it. And believe it or not, Grandda doesn't care for it at all."

"As much as he loves sweets, chocolate has never been his favorite flavor. He prefers things with whipped topping and plenty of ice cream." They both laughed. "Chris is buying out every shop we go by. And we've picked up a few things for the babies too. We're going to hit a show tonight and dinner before heading back to the hotel."

"I had hoped that it wasn't going to be just a working trip for the two of you and that you'd have some fun. And before I forget, I have a list of things I'm supposed to let you know about that's going on at your ranch. Elwood misses you, but since Chris talked to him before she left, he's eating but pouting." Joey laughed. "Also, the house is fine. It was sweet of you to have Grandda and Grandma stay there for you. I think they're having a good time being substitute ranchers. Heath is taking care that they don't get into trouble, and Drew is keeping an eye on things around the place. Also, Carol Lewis is putting up a fuss. The sheriff is saying he's about ready to ship her home

Anthony

on his own. I assured him that you'd take care of it when you returned. This was family business."

"Thank you. She has a court appearance a few days after we return, and I'm going to make sure that she gets what she deserves. It won't be what she wants, but it will make all of us happy anyway." He saw Chris in line to check out, and groaned when he saw all the bags she'd filled around her. "We might have to buy stock in this place. It might be cheaper than having her come out here to buy things. But she is having fun if nothing else. I have to get some things for Micah while I'm here too. Did you know that there is a big sex shop here?"

"I heard, and if you get me something naughty, you'd better get one for your wife as well. If not, then I'm going to tell on you." He told her he would for sure. "Also, you should know that I think we're going to take a short vacation when this all settles. Micah is going to ask you to keep an eye on the leap for us. Can you?"

"Yes. I can do that. But you'll owe me. I wonder what I could ask for?" She suggested something. "No, I don't think that would be overly fun for me. Sticking a stick up my already tight ass sounds like something that you might like."

Reggie was still laughing when he closed his phone. Walking into the store, he reached for his driver and asked him to meet them out front when he could manage it. He told him twenty minutes and Joey thanked him. Joey kissed Chris and put his hand on her large belly. The babies stretched under his hand when he did.

"You get anything for us?" She nodded and laid her head on his shoulder. "Are you tired, love? The car is coming to get

153

some of our things; we can go back to the hotel for a nap if you want."

"I think I would like that." He nodded and helped her move ahead in line. "Then I'd very much like to have a huge dinner afterwards. I heard of several places that have the best food."

"It's Vegas, love. You can't help but have great food." She laughed, but he could tell she was really tiring. "I'll finish up here. Why don't you have a seat over there, and when the car comes I'll load you into it, and then run you a nice bath when we get to the hotel. Then while you're lying down, I'll massage your poor feet."

"I'd love that." The woman behind them sighed and Chris looked at her with a smile. "He's the best, isn't he? A woman couldn't have it better than me."

"I believe you. I do. And a man who will massage your feet after shopping, he's a keeper." He and Chris laughed. "You go on over there, honey. I'll hold his place in line until he gets you settled. When you due?"

"Two months." The woman looked at her belly, then at him, like she was sizing up how large their child was going to be. "We're going to have twins, but no one knows yet."

"Honey, I'm pretty sure that everyone knows that you're big for a single baby. Even with the size of your husband, you're big. Congratulations. Now you go have a rest. And I'll hold this place for you like I said."

As Joey moved to the seat with Chris, he decided that he was as happy as he could be. When he got back, he was next in line and told the cashier that he would pay for the woman who was behind him as well. It was the least he could do for such a nice person.

Chris napped on the ride back. As soon as they were out of the car, he had the driver take the things to the plane and have them loaded. There was no point in crowding the rooms when they had a perfectly good storage unit on standby. Chris was asleep almost as soon as she laid down. The bath had been too much, she said, but he did massage her feet and ankles. While he wasn't scared for her, he did reach out to his brothers to see if she was doing all right.

Twins. Burke laughed when he told him that was right. *We had bets, Nolan and I. He said three. But I thought twins. And as far along as she is, being tired a lot is more normal than having this much exhaustion with a single birth.*

And make sure that she's drinking enough while there. The air is drier, and she might be slightly dehydrated. He was making notes on what Nolan said to him as well. *Let her nap when she needs to. You know her as well as she does herself. Even if she tells you she's all right, have her sit more often, take care that she's eating well, and for the love of everything, make sure that you tell her that you think she's beautiful.*

She is beautiful. And I tell her that all the time. Nolan explained. *Oh. She may be feeling that she isn't. Okay, I get it. I do think she's the most beautiful woman in the world, pregnant or not.*

They talked for a bit more. Nolan told him that he was headed out to Bentley's, the name that they'd finally decided on for the restaurant, to have a look at the crowds, and Burke told him that he and Pip were actually going to have dinner there tonight. They'd been fully booked for over a week now, and poor Coleen was beside herself. And Tony was as well.

He's holding up well, I think. He asked Burke why he thought he wouldn't. *His mate is about to debut as one of the premier chefs in the state, and he's running around like a chicken with his head cut off because she asked him to host for her tonight. You'd think that she asked him to sub cook for her; he's so afraid he'll make her look bad. Poor guy. I thought we were going to have to sedate him when he came by to ask if his suit was good enough. I have to tell you, I laugh about it still.*

Good for her. Joey laughed along with his brothers. *I'm glad she made him dress up. I have never seen a man so turned off by wearing a tux. I kinda like them. In fact, I'm wearing one tonight. Chris and I have dinner reservations at five, then we're off to see a show at seven-thirty.* Both brothers cautioned him again about the fluids, as well as resting. *I promise. I'll make sure she does both, and that she keeps her feet up too. And maybe when this is finished here, we can just come on home. Vegas is really nice, but it's not Ohio.*

He was reviewing what he wanted to go over in the morning meeting when Chris came out of the bedroom. She looked better, and when she went to the little fridge and got a bottle of water, he leaned back and watched her.

"My brothers?" She nodded as she drank from the bottle. "I was concerned about you being so tired. I did point out to them that we'd walked a great deal, but they said it was a drier air out here and you might not be drinking enough. I ordered juice to be sent up as well. I just have to let them know when you want it."

"Almost as soon as I opened my eyes they both pounced on me. I'm glad that they're concerned, but they should give a girl a moment to fully wake up." He got up and sat beside her

156

on the couch before pulling her onto his lap. "Thank you for being my mate. And for taking such good care of me. There is no telling what sort of trouble I'd get into without you."

"You're so very welcome. And I live for you being a bad girl. Also, thank you for being a witch." A lot of what was going on tomorrow morning depended on her ability to not be lied to, and the fact that she could see into their minds. They weren't going to manipulate things—that could have major repercussions—but they could figure out a lot just by simply being themselves. "We don't have to go anywhere tonight if you just want to stay here."

"I do want to go." He nodded. "I suppose you have a really expensive place all picked out, and that I'm going to be waddling around like this well after the babies are here."

"Yes. But I want you to know that I think you are the most beautiful creature I've ever had the pleasure of being around. As far as waddling, you don't now." He put his hand on her belly and felt the babies move. It was as if they knew it was Dad, and they were reaching out to him. "As much as I'd like to sit here and hold you, if we're going to be on time, we have to get ready. And I have something for you."

He reached between the cushions of the couch and handed her the long blue box. He'd put it there when they'd gotten back to make sure he gave it to her for tonight. When she opened it, he watched her face. The bracelet had been specially made for her, and he needed to know that she loved it.

The chain was as delicate as she was. Each of the charms on it, all the same gold as the chain, had a special meaning to them. He had worked hard on each one of them, and hoped she understood their meaning.

"Elwood." He nodded at the horse he'd had fashioned after the big animal. As she went through all ten of them, he told her what they meant to him as well. The ruby heart was his that she held inside of her. The small bassinets, one with a blue sapphire, the other a pink diamond, were for their children. There was a wand for her magic that had a bright diamond at its top. Their home was there too, in a much smaller version, and then there was the ring that he removed from the clasp.

"I wanted you to have this because not a minute goes by that I don't think of you in even the smallest of ways. The way you breathe in and out. When I hear your heart beating under my ear after we've made love." He slipped the ring onto a finger on her right hand. "I love you, Chris, with all that I am, and will for the rest of our lives."

"I love you as well."

She leaned her head on his shoulder and cried softly. He knew it was hormones that made her so touchy, but it tore at him all the same. When she was better, she stood up and told him it was time they got going. Joey thought himself the luckiest man in the entire world.

~~~

The menus were perfect now, checked four times after they'd figured out that she'd spelled Bentley wrong on the first one. She'd been nervous, but that hadn't stopped the teasing. They decided that they'd print one up nightly with the specials, and have the rest already in the new menu holders, things that they were going to serve all the time. There wasn't much — three appetizers and two salads to choose from — but they did have

158

some things that would not change. And they had decided against a children's section, for no other reason than it would need to be too varied for a child's tastes.

"I think we're ready." Coleen looked up as Tansy spoke. "You look like you're going to throw up. Are you okay?"

"Yes and no. I just want this to be done, don't you?" Tansy nodded and grinned at her. "You're going to do well. I'm not concerned about you or Matt, but there are a lot of reservations. Did you see them?"

"I did. I think it's wonderful for your first night open." Coleen rubbed her belly. "Once the orders start coming in, you'll be fine, you told us. And we're counting on that. But right now, you're just thinking about all the things that could go wrong. I don't think there is a better prepared place than we are. We are going to make this shit happen."

Which was true. The trout was all ready and in individual dishes ready to be baked. The hens, all of them cooked and ready to be put in the oven again to be readied with the sauce over them, were in the warming ovens. Even the pork was ready for just the sauce and the grilled fruit. Coleen went over the list again, this time with Tansy there to help.

"I have all of the gnocchi ready too, measured out so that we can just drop them into water to cook. And the desserts are beautiful, all sliced and ready to be served up. The whipped topping is done, and if it needs to be freshened when needed, everything is ready. A bowl of dark chocolate all shaved prettily is in the small refrigerator, and there are chopped nuts if they need them as well." At Tansy's words, Coleen nodded. She had been working since last night on those, and Tansy had praised her all day on them. "Howie will be a little miffed that he didn't get to taste them all, but we should be okay if we save him a slice or two of the apple tarts I made this morning."

"He'll be here, and I'm sure that he'll have enough to eat." Tansy said she wasn't so sure. "Do you really think that people are going to hang around for desserts after they eat?"

"I hope they don't in a way. We have a huge turnover tonight, and we need to clean up the tables out there. Oh, and you were right in suggesting that Betty be in charge of the floor. She's got everyone dressed and pressed." Coleen nodded. It had been one less thing she had to worry about. "And Pip sent over flowers for everyone to wear on their tops so that we match the rest of the décor. I love it."

The wait staff was partly high school kids and adults. While they didn't have a bar, they did have a wine list. It had been something that Rylee had suggested a few days ago, so getting in some different kinds had been a rush. They had ten of each kind that Micah and Burke had looked up on the Internet to accompany different kinds of meat. She'd been using one or two of them in the kitchen to cook with, and liked most of them. Coleen made her way into the kitchen to make sure they were as ready as they'd been ten minutes ago when she'd checked.

Ten minutes before five, when they were supposed to open, Betty came back and asked if she could start seating. They were lined up, she told her, and it was sort of cold out. Nodding, Coleen told her to tell them that they'd need a bit of time to get warm bread to them; a table treat, Howie called it, to soothe the beasts. Betty said that she would and left them. Twenty minutes later, they were busy.

Coleen never stopped to think about what they were doing. An order came in and they filled it and sent it out again. The wait staff seemed to be enjoying what they were doing, telling them that people were having fun. One of them, a kid saving money for his college tuition in the fall, was so happy to have such nice tips that he danced around the kitchen until Betty put a stop to it. Coleen was smiling still when the order came in for Burke and Pip.

The staff had been told that if a family member came in they were to mark the orders accordingly. They weren't going to get anything different than the rest of the patrons, but she wanted to know who was coming in. As his order was put on the grill, trout for him and hen for Pip, she thought of the million and a half things she was going to have to do when they were done. Glancing at the clock, she stared at it for a full minute when she realized how long they'd been cooking. Betty came back again and asked if she could seat a party of two since it was past closing time.

"Yes. Let me see what we have left." It was twenty after ten. A full hour later than they were supposed to close when she came back from the walk-in. "I have two of each meal, as well as plenty of everything else. Bread is just coming out, so can you take that with you?"

Betty said she would, and once the bread was sliced up and stacked in the basket, she left them. When the order came in, she didn't think of anything but that they'd made it through the night without anyone getting hurt or poisoned. Coleen told Tansy and Matt that they could make themselves dinner, and to make sure that the staff was fed as well.

161

The table ordered one of each meal. It was sort of odd, but she knew that some other tables had done the same thing to share. She didn't care. It would be less that they'd have to contend with at the end of the night. Coleen cooked the entire thing herself as the rest of them started to break down the serving tables that they'd used for the night. The salads were put away, the bread that hadn't been baked was put in the freezer. And any of the cooked food, green beans and such, were given to the staff to take home if they wanted. Coleen didn't care for serving leftovers, and wouldn't start it at this point in her career.

She felt really good about what they'd all done tonight. Not one meal had come back, the dirty plates looked cleaned, and no one had sent back a single complaint about how long some meals were taking. Just the trout, but that had been something that she'd gone over with the staff to tell the patrons.

At just after eleven, Tony came back to get her. "There is a couple here that want to meet you. The last ones you served." She looked around to see if she could send someone else out — it was what she'd done earlier — and he shook his head. "They want to meet you. They asked for Coleen Bentley."

"I don't want to go." He laughed and took her by the hand, giving her just enough time to change into a clean coat. Hers had been stained almost from the beginning. As she made sure she was cleaned up, she glanced at Tony in the mirror. "Who are these people, anyway?"

"I'm not sure. They were really nice when I seated them. And raved about the bread and butter as soon as they sat down." Tony kissed her on the nose. "So you know, I'm going to ravage you when we get home tonight."

Anthony

"You are at that." As soon as they were in the dining area, she saw that all the tables that were empty had been reset, the glasses turned up so they didn't give the appearance of being closed, as well as fresh flowers were at the tables that the patrons were being encouraged to take when they left. Pip had thought it would be a lovely parting gift.

"Mrs. Bentley?" She took the man's hand when he offered his. "I'm so very glad to meet you. I've been completely blown away by tonight's dinner, and just had to talk to you before we left."

"Thank you. We've been having some test drives on things and having a good time." He laughed and asked her what a test drive was. "Sorry. My grandfather-in-law. He calls getting to help us out by sampling things for us a test drive. It's sort of stuck. He's been most helpful on things before we opened our doors. Not that he's found too much that he wouldn't eat, but if you met him, you'd understand."

"I should think that you being at the helm has made it easy for him to enjoy his driving too." She nodded and sat down when he offered her a seat. "I'm to understand that you were never a starred chef before this."

"No. I worked in a lot of places and was saving up for a place of my own. But I came here to live with my grandma to help her out, and this opportunity came about. The Bentleys have been very supportive, and I couldn't have done this without them." He just nodded. "I'm very glad that you enjoyed your dinners. We will have a different one nightly when we're open full time. Tonight was a grand opening, and for the rest of the week we'll regroup and figure out what we're doing wrong and fix it."

"I'm sure that there can't be too many things you have to adjust. Unless it's to add a table or two more. After tonight, I think you might want to think of expanding your seating. This is a lovely place, and you've done well all the way around." She thanked him again. "My wife and I, we travel around to different restaurants all the time. It was a fluke that we found ourselves here on this night. I'm very glad that our plane had a little trouble and we got to be here."

"I'm glad as well." When they stood up to leave, she and Tony did as well. "Whenever you're in town again, I do hope that you'll join us. We would love to have you."

"I believe you are sincere about that." Coleen looked at Tony, confused, then the man laughed at her. "You have a lovely evening, my dear. You deserve it. And I have your company email address as well."

"Thank you." After they left, she asked Tony what that was about, and he only grinned at her. "You're being very strange; you know that, don't you?"

"Yes. But now that you're finished up here, I'd like to take you up on that deal to run you down in the woods. I know it's cold, but I think I can warm you up." Her body was warm now, and he inhaled deeply. "I can smell you. You're very aroused, aren't you?"

"I am."

She went to check on the kitchen, and found that not only was everything cleaned up, but the staff was gone as well. Gathering up the money bag without looking at it, she made her way to the front of the restaurant with Tony and locked up. After making the deposit, they drove home. Coleen had her own plans tonight.

Tonight she'd become a cat. After talking with both Burke and Nolan about what to expect, she knew it was going to be painful, but it would be worth it. Both of them told her that she should talk it over with Tony, and she was going to, but at the last minute. Nothing was going to keep her from this. She needed this as much as he did. Smiling, she stripped off her coat and threw it in the back of the car as soon as they stopped at the house, and then took off running. Coleen was excited about a great many things about tonight.

Anthony

CHAPTER 11

Tony knew what she was about. Burke had told him, then Nolan had come by his offices to let him know as well. They didn't want to betray her trust, but they wanted to make sure he knew that she might be hurt more than any of them might anticipate. He was going to tease her relentlessly before he converted her. Letting his panther take him, Tony followed her scent into the deep dark woods.

It's really fucking cold. How the hell do you get used to all this snow? It's like an ice box all the time. He laughed and told her it was winter. *Yeah, I get that, but I thought it would be warmer by now for some reason. I mean, it is mid-February, for heaven's sake. I guess being in a hot kitchen all night can make the temps feel colder than it really is.*

I think it's nine degrees right now. She thanked him for that bit of information. *You're welcome. Would you like to know who that man was that you sat with tonight?*

Just some nice man, right? And he was. Did you know that he ordered one of each of the meals tonight, and an extra portion of gnocchi? I didn't know if I would have enough, but apparently he was happy with it. He told her that was what he wanted her to believe, that he was just a nice man. *I don't care unless he was some critic that is going to write something up about me tomorrow.*

Tony paused when he saw her and waited for her to say more. *Tony? That was all he was, right? A nice man? One that was really hungry and not trying out the dishes so he could write about them?*

He is very nice, yes. And you are correct about the rest as well. She asked him what he meant. *He is a critic that is going to write you up in his article tomorrow. I see you. You should try and hide better. This won't be very sporting if you don't hide better.*

She came out of her hiding place and just stood there. He could feel her anxiety and could see it on her face. When she asked him where he was, he lifted his head and told her to turn to him.

"Tell me you're kidding me. Please?" He only watched her. "Why on earth didn't you tell me before I went out there and made a fool of myself? And good heavens, he ate all we served tonight. I think I'm going to be sick."

No, you're not. You did very well, and everyone could see that. He did too. He enjoyed it all, including you. And the wine that he had. I told you he loved the bread as soon as he sat down. She sat down and he went to her. *I'm sorry, baby. I'm pretty sure that he's going to give you a good review.*

"I don't want any review. I just wanted to have some fun." He nuzzled her neck and licked her there. "I'm not in the mood right now. You set me up."

I did nothing of the kind. He nipped harder at her throat and moaned when she rubbed her hand over his back. *I'd like to have you lay back on the ground naked for us so we can taste you. Then when he's had his fill, I'd like to fuck you hard enough to have you scream.*

"You always make me scream. Even when I know that everyone in the house can hear me. I think about that sometimes, how loud I am, and wonder why Daniel hasn't quit. Or asked you if I was insane." She laid back when he nudged her again. "You should know that I was planning to make you change me tonight. I want it badly."

I know that, darling. Take off your clothing for me. Standing up, he watched her strip. Her body was cold, her nipples hard stones, and all he could think about was taking them into his mouth. When she laid back, he settled between her legs and took his body back. He wanted to talk to her, face to face, about what they were about to do. "When I bite you, it's going to be painful. I know that you talked to Burke and Nolan, but I want you to know that once I start, if I stop before it's taken effect, you'll die."

"I know." She touched his face, then reached down to stroke his cock with her nimble fingers. "I want this. Very much so. I can't stand not being like you. Do it now, Tony. Convert me so that the next time we come out here in the woods, I can run with you."

Kissing her, showing her with his mouth how much he loved her, he lifted his head and his cat took him. This time there wasn't any fooling around; he lunged for her belly and bit down hard enough to penetrate her stomach. And so it begins, he told himself. She would be his cat, and he'd love her all the more for it. If he didn't kill her first.

Her scream tore at his heart and mind. Tony knew that it was going to hurt her, that she'd scream, but it made it no less painful to him. When she put her hand on his head, he felt his cat purr loudly and she laughed a little.

"You are wonderful for doing this for me. I want to be a pretty kitty too, just like you are." He told her he loved her. "I love you as well. Now what? Where next? They told me, but I'm a little fuzzy on the details right now."

Your thigh, then your throat. You won't hurt so badly at your neck. She didn't ask him why, so he didn't bother telling her that she'd be out by then. Or at least he hoped she would be. *I love you so very much, Coleen. And I cannot wait for you to wake on the other side of this.*

The next bite to her thigh had her sitting up and pulling at his fur. Not like she was trying to pull him away, but like she was hanging onto him. His cat tore at her flesh; then, making the bite deeper, he felt the bones break under the pressure. When she fell back, limp, and her eyes closed, he knew that he'd never want to do this to anyone ever again. Tasting the difference in her blood, he moved up to her throat and bit there as well, drawing out her blood and taking it into his own body to complete the circle. She was panther as of now. His cat, and a true member of the leap that his family was in. Micah would be happy as well.

While her body was still working on being converted, he laid over her, his body keeping hers warm until she was complete. The sun was cresting over the trees when he lifted his body from hers and shifted back to man. Picking her up,

Anthony

unmindful of the fact that they were both naked, he took her to the house and to their room. He was glad that no one had seen him as he made his way through their home. This was something private, something for the two of them to share. And he was glad now that she'd taken it upon herself to have him do this tonight.

Laying her on their bed, he ran a bath for her, knowing that she'd rest better if she was cleaned up. He lifted her once again and lowered the two of them into the tub even as the water level seemed to never change. It wasn't until they were submerged to their shoulders that he realized that the tub was accommodating them in this. He thanked the house for its help. Washing her hair of the sticks and leaves, he told her all the things that he loved about her.

"You never say you can't. I never noticed that until Tansy pointed it out. You might say that you'll give it your best or that you'll figure it out, but you don't say you won't be able to do whatever it is you've set your mind to." He pulled a dried leaf from her hair as he continued. "Also how protective you are of my family. My grandda especially. He notices it too. And you have no idea how proud he is of the fact that even though he's a cat and can kill without hesitation, you are forever in front of whatever he might find himself into. And believe me when I tell you, that's a lot of the time. And he is very excited that you're going to go fishing with him and the boys this summer. He can be the most annoying man, but the most loving as well. My mom thinks of you as her daughter, just as she does the others. There is no in-law in her family, she told me."

He rinsed her hair of all the suds and smiled at something

else he remembered. "The critic. He was so in awe of you. Your first night open and he got to see you in action. And you really impressed him with how you kept saying it was a team effort and that family helped you. He loved how you were so modest about things. Real, he called you in his thoughts. I think that was what impressed him the most; you were so down to earth about what was going on." He was going to have to have someone send him copies of the NYT, so he could frame a few hundred copies. It never occurred to him that she'd get anything but a good review. Even three stars would be nice...this first time anyway.

When she was cleaned up, he pushed the button on the tub to let the water out and sat her on the counter to dry her off. As soon as he'd done the best he could, he picked her up again and put her in bed. The covers were pulled back for her and the pillows were fluffed up. Smiling, he dried himself off and crawled into bed beside her. Tony reached out to Micah to let him know that he'd done it.

Good. I'm glad to hear it. By the way, I just heard from a friend of mine at the Times. Did you know that someone was in the restaurant last night to review her? Tony said they'd met him, but Coleen didn't know until later who he was. *Do you want me to read you what it says? It's impressive to say the least.*

No. I'd like to see it with Coleen. Can you send over a few copies so we can read them when she wakes up? He said that he'd do that. *Also, can you let Burke and Nolan know, as well as the rest of them, that things went as well as they said they would. She was hurt, but she came through it like she'd done it a million times before. Tell them that we love them and that we'll be resting up for a few days.*

Take care, and I'm very happy for you both. Tony yawned and thanked Micah as he curled around Coleen. *I'll see you in a few days then. Call me if you need anything.*

I will. Closing his eyes, he thought of something else. *I have something at the jewelers in town. Can you pick it up for me and bring it around when you have time? It's paid for, just needs to be picked up.*

It would be my pleasure. Good night, little brother.

Tony felt sleep take him even before he could answer Micah. He was going to marry her as soon as he could arrange it, and now he had the ring to do so.

~~~

Chris wanted to get up and hit someone. Namely the men on the other side of the door that had been closed to them. She had lost her patience with the lot of them when they'd made them wait for over an hour so far to get into their offices. Their excuse had been that they needed to read over phone messages. The secretary was beside herself with nervousness. Chris knew that she was aware of what they were, and tried twice now to reassure her that everything on her end was going to be fine.

"I'm not here to see you, I told you that. Please don't be upset." She nodded, but still would make no eye contact with her. "You're just fine. Just do what you normally do and things will come out all right."

"They're underhanded and cruel. But I'm pretty sure you know that already, don't you, my lady?" Chris asked her if they knew what she was, a witch of high marks, and a white one as she was. "I think they do. I'm teased constantly, and every week on Friday I have a witch of some sort on my desk. It's getting really old."

173

"I'll take care of it." The woman nodded. "When we go into their offices, would you please do me a favor and see what you can find on other cases like the one that has my sister-in-law in hock to her ass? I have a feeling that they've been up to this for some time."

The young witch reached into her drawer and handed her a notebook. Before Chris could ask her what it was, she laid an envelope on the desk and picked up her purse. Smiling at the three of them, the woman walked out of the area and to the elevator. Chris would bet anything that the men in this office would miss that woman more than they might their right nut. Chris opened the notebook and smiled.

There was a list of fifty-two names. File numbers, as well as cross references on other files. There were also three CD type discs in the back, and a copy of her resignation. Handing everything to the man sitting to her right, she told Joey what it was.

"She knew this day was coming. And she was prepared for it." William Taylor, the man she'd given the notebook to, got up and went out of the little area they were in. "He's going to find someone to get those for us, I'm betting. I think he has a cat or two here that he can command to do it."

"I don't doubt that. From what Reggie told me, he has one of the largest leaps in the world here. And there are over seven hundred of them in some type of law work alone." Chris smiled and wanted to get up and pace. As soon as she stood, Joey handed her a bottle of water. "I'm going to keep giving you those until we leave here. You're not going to get sick on me."

"I won't. I want to go home too." As she paced, he looked

over the file he'd brought with them. It wasn't going to be necessary, she thought. Once she got in there, she was going to zap them both to hell. Not really, but she was going to hurt them if they didn't get their act together.

When William came back, she turned when the door finally opened. William was nearly glowing with good humor. She had to smile with him. The shit was about to be a nasty mess all over those two men who dared to fuck with her family.

"I just came out to tell you that things are running longer than we anticipated. You can either come back tomorrow or we can see you in about another hour or so. I'm terribly sorry." He looked at the desk, then frowned. "I was going to have Sally show you where you can go to the conference room, but she must have stepped out."

"I think she quit." Joey stood up when he spoke. "And if you try and take us to another room to have us cool our heels there, I'm not going to be at all happy with you. I think you've made us wait long enough."

Joey moved by the man and into the big office. Chris was right behind him, with William bringing up the rear. George Conley, the head of this firm, only huffed at them as he sat behind his desk. Harry Mercer was seated already, and didn't even rise when they came into the room. Chris thought this was going to be a good deal more fun than she'd hoped for. At least for her anyway.

"I have no idea why you're here. I don't even know who you are. My secretary said that it was a matter that you would explain when you got here. Well? I've a very busy schedule this week, and if you could just explain, we'll help you in any way that we can." Chris sat down and watched both men carefully. "I'm sorry. What did you say your names were?"

"We didn't, but I'm Joey Bentley. This is my wife, Chris, and our friend, William. We've come on the matter of Greer versus the State of Nevada. We're concerned about some of the bills that we've been looking into for her." Both men seemed to freeze up. Then George smiled. "You are aware of the case, aren't you?"

"Oh yes. We're aware of it. She already signed off on the paperwork to begin paying us a great amount of money. I'm looking forward to getting her first payment. I'm to understand that she's landed a very nice job. Good for her. She'll have us paid in no time now." He reached into his desk and pulled out a thick file. "But there are a few more that we just found to add to her billing. We've come across other bills that we want to have her pay us for. And since she didn't sleep with either of us, we're going to send her a bill for our services. There wasn't any reason for her to run off the same day we took her for everything she owns."

He looked around, as if he wasn't sure why he'd said that. Chris had only snapped her fingers, and now no one in the room could lie to her or Joey. It was the only way they figured they'd get to the bottom of this mess.

"I have no idea why I said that. What I meant to say was we found a way to get rich fast, and she's only a small fish in a big pond." George put his hand over his mouth and looked panicky. "What's going on here?"

"You can't lie to us, no matter what. And no, I don't think you'll be adding anything to what you've scammed her out of.

176

I think you're going to be lucky if we only take what you have in your accounts." George started to speak, but Joey continued and cut him off. "I have two billings here that I'd like to start with. This one that has no amount on it that just says 'whatever' in the total column. Is that your handwriting?"

"No, it's Harry's. He had to go to great links to get those printed up that way." Again he looked around the room. "What I mean is, he had to find a way to get a blank billing so that we could put any amount we wanted in so that the unsuspecting client wouldn't know the difference. How did you get this copy?"

"You'd be surprised what a person can find when they look hard enough. This particular blank bill has shown up in several other cases that you had where the deceased left behind a great many bills, hasn't it?" George looked at Harry like he was trying not to say anything. "I asked you a question. Did you use this particular scam on other clients to overbill them and to pocket the difference?"

"Yes." George got up and began pacing. "I don't like where this is going. And I have no idea how you're making me not lie to you, but I want you to stop it. You're making me look bad, and I don't care for that. I think it's about time that you left, all of you. There is something going on, and I'll have to have it looked into."

"I'm not ready to leave just yet. Not until I have some answers. By making you look bad, do you mean that you've been lying to a great many people all along?" Again George said yes. "I see. Do you have any idea how much you've made on this particular scam? By the way, you are aware that it's against the law, aren't you? Not to mention unethical, and something that will get you a long prison sentence."

"Only if we're caught. Listen, these people should know better than to trust a lawyer. I mean, we're all thieves, aren't we?" Joey told him he wasn't, nor was his wife. "Yes, well, I guess you're the minority then. But it's not that big of a deal. Most of these people are deadbeats anyway. And they eventually end up killing themselves trying to pay back this money. Why shouldn't we make a little off them? We don't even charge for going to court with them. Unless they're not willing to put out, which your sister-in-law did not. And when they don't, we bill them and they come around. I've yet to hear from Coleen. Is she going to come here and have sex with us?"

"No, she's not, and if I were you, I'd not mention that again. But back to this billing; you mean you go out and agree to represent these people, when you know for a fact that you're going to lie and cheat them?" George nodded, and so did Harry this time when William asked them. "And again, you knew this was against the law, yet you did it anyway. Don't you know that you're breaking every law that you promised to uphold?"

"We made sure that the person was dead so they'd not be able to go and check on the bills. What harm does it do for us to make some money off them?" William told them plenty of harm. "I don't know what's going on here, but you people aren't what I expected. You should be happy about what we're doing here. Taking the scum of the earth off the streets and making sure they get jobs. Of course they pay a lot to us, but they do have jobs."

Harry went to the door and opened it. "I agree with George.

You guys need to leave. And don't come back. You're making us say things that can get us into trouble, and I don't care for it. Not one bit."

Joey just looked at Chris and smiled. William got up but he didn't move to the door. Instead, he picked up the file on the desk and begin looking through it. George tried to snatch it from him, but he was ordered to stay put.

"This is a travesty. I mean, worse than that, this is outrageous. You've been stealing from your clients for…well, how long?" Harry answered. "Ten years. You've been pulling this shit for ten years, and we're just now finding out about it?"

"People are stupid. And who were we hurting, anyway? A bunch of deadbeats that should have known better than to marry in the first place. And as I have pointed out, they're working now. That should be enough for you to get off our backs." Joey got up, and Chris had a moment of fear when he jerked Harry from his position at the door and lifted him up by his neck. As he struggled to breathe, William moved around the desk and touched his arm.

"I have it from here, Joey. Trust me, they'll make restitution on this." Joey held Harry for a few seconds longer before he tossed him across the room. William sat at George's desk and told them to have a seat.

"In the event that you might have missed something, this is my office and I will say who comes or goes, and you three are going to get out of here. I've worked very hard to get where I am, and I plan to stay here until I have enough. In fact, I'm calling security now." George picked up the phone and told whoever was on the other end what he needed before hanging up. "I don't know who you people are, but you cannot come into a person's office and accuse them of cheating people like you have. We have, but really, who cares anyway? You can bet I'm going to be taking this to someone who can take care of the three of you as soon as you're gone."

"Well, aren't you just a lucky fuck today. I'm William Taylor, States Attorney for the State of Nevada. This is Joseph Bentley, attorney for his sister-in-law, Coleen Greer Bentley, and this young woman is Joey's wife, Chris Bentley, also an attorney. You are so fucked right now, George, you're going to be lucky if you ever see the light of day again. And you too, Harry. Right off the top of my head, I can think of about ten thousand things that are going to get you a very long prison term."

When security was at the door, Chris told them to wait. None of them seemed too surprised to see a stranger at the desk, nor did they question her when she asked them to call the police. One of them, a wolf, stood at the door when his boss, the head of security, went to use the phone in the outer office to make the call. Chris asked the wolf if the young secretary had made it out of the building all right.

"Yes, ma'am, Sally did. She said that the shit...crap was about to hit the fan, and that we'd be better served to listen to you and the mister rather than doing anything that Conley might tell us." She told him that might be a wonderful idea all around. "He's been telling us for months now that we're all going to be kissing his ass soon enough. I'd just like to see him kicked out on it."

"He will be." The guard just nodded. "I'd like for you to

gather up everyone that works here and have them go to the large conference room on the second floor and wait. Tell them that the police will be along shortly."

He asked her if they'd be all right. "Crow—my boss, Mr. Crow—he wants to make sure that you don't get hurt should they take out the guns." She asked him where they were. "In the top drawer of his desk. I've already taken Mr. Mercer's. Just as soon as we got the call."

"Good job. And I'm sure that Sally told you what we are?" He nodded and seemed slightly nervous. "I think we can handle anything that he might try to dish out. You go on and gather them up. And if anyone tries to leave, you call me."

She touched her fingers to the back of his hand. When he looked at her she knew that this man was as terrified of her as he was of anything else he'd seen in this office. After assuring him that he'd be just fine, she'd make sure of it, he left to do as she'd told him. When Crow returned, she did the same for him, then sent him to the conference rooms. They'd be safer there, and until the police arrived no one would be able to sneak out. Chris knew there were several people in this building that were helping Mercer and Conley, and profiting off it as well.

After the first hour it became apparent that there was more going on than they'd thought. Not only were they bilking people with the billing scam, but there were hundreds of millions of dollars' worth of over billing, mail fraud, as well as a great many other things that simply boggled her mind. How long did they think this could go on before someone caught up to them? Apparently for a long time.

While she worked at the desk finding all the money that

the two of them had stashed all over the world, the IRS came in and started questioning the staff. Another group was sent to the two men's homes, where things were taken and bagged up. Chris leaned back in the seat when someone suggested they order some dinner.

"I'm sorry." She looked up at Joey and smiled. "I had no idea it was going to be this long. I would have left you at the hotel had I thought it would be."

"I wouldn't have stayed. This is important to both of us." He nodded and sat down. "Has anyone heard from Tony about Coleen? I was wondering if she's still resting."

"She was when I spoke to him an hour ago. Do me a favor and pull up today's Times. I guess there is a review of her restaurant in it." Chris did a search and pulled it up. As she read it aloud to Joey, she had to smile. "This is fantastic. And expected. She's an amazing chef, and I've never eaten better anywhere. Have you?"

"No, I haven't. She's not going to be happy about this. I think her plan was to be more low key on things for a bit longer." Joey said that was certainly out the door. "I think you might be right. Has Tony seen it yet?"

"No, Micah told him about it, but he said he didn't want to know what the guy said about the place until he could share it with Coleen. Tony did tell her about the critic being there before he converted her, but nothing more." She read the rest of the article. "Well, he seemed to like her style and cooking. That doesn't surprise me either. Especially after how she treated Elroy when he came to the restaurant that day. She welcomed him, when I'm betting he'd not have done the same for her."

182

"I know you're right about that. But in reading this, I think the critic was enamored of her, if you ask me." Chris laughed as she shut down the article and looked at Joey. "How about we finish up here, go back to the hotel, pack, and go home? I miss our bed."

"I miss the family too." He kissed her and started for the door. "Joey, when we get home, I'd like for you to do me a favor."

"Anything love, you name it." She nodded, knowing that he'd say that to her. "You know I love you more than anything in this world, and would do anything at all to make you happy."

"I know. That's why I love you so much." He asked her what she needed. "I want to help Coleen expand her restaurant. I think after this, she's going to need more space than she ever thought possible."

Joey was still laughing when he went out the door. Chris thought perhaps he believed her, but didn't think she'd need it this soon. Chris knew better. Once people started hearing about Bentley's and the antique store, as well as the large nursery, their little town was going to be bursting with people. They might even need to get a few more shops opened as well.

Anthony

CHAPTER 12

Coleen stood under the spray for ten minutes. The water was drowning out some of the noise that seemed to be echoing in her head, but not all of it. She'd been told that she would hear and smell things better, but they never mentioned being able to hear a fly breathing on a banana four hundred miles away. It wasn't that bad, but it was really loud.

When someone touched her arm, she screamed and lashed out. Tony just stepped back from her when she realized that her hand was covered in dark fur and had sprouted claws. She looked at him when he said her name. Coleen promptly burst into tears.

"It's all right, baby. You must not have heard me saying your name." She told him about the fly and the banana. "Well, that fly was pretty noisy. I had Awnia kick his ass out. The banana is ruined by the way…we had to give it a nice burial in the yard."

"Don't make fun of me." He handed her a towel and then dried her hair while she wrapped the other around her. "I thought you'd left me for the day. I woke up and my head felt like it was on fire, so I came in here to try to muffle the noises."

"I heard the shower turn on and started to come up, but I thought you'd be down soon. I should have come up sooner, but Chris and Joey are back." She asked him what they'd found out. "I was just coming up to get you to see if you wanted to hear it too."

"Yes." She grabbed the brush and was dragging it through her hair when she turned to him. "How long was I out? It couldn't have been that long, was it?"

"Three days. It's Wednesday. So not too bad. How do you feel?" She looked at her hand, which was normal again, and told him she was a little afraid. "When they leave we'll go out in the back and you can shift. You'll feel better once you have her come to you. And you'll feel more in control as well. It's a lot to get used to. But I have to say, you have the defense part of it down." She told him to fuck off.

Pulling on clothing, she could hear each scrape of the material over her skin. When she complained to Tony, he told her to think of a volume knob on a stereo and turn it down. It was the way he'd heard a male wolf describe how to do it a long time ago. Closing her eyes, she did just what he said, and then looked at him.

"It worked." He nodded and she smiled. "I feel really good. I mean, energized and everything. Will I be able to heal now too?" Tony told her she'd be able to do a great many things. "The healing thing is what I'm most excited about, I think. Everything, really. The running in the woods. Knowing that I have this other part of me that is only mine. I know that sounds really selfish, but it's wonderful knowing that.

"It's not selfish at all. I have the same feelings. It's also empowering, knowing that you can keep yourself and the ones around you a little safer because you have this stronger other self." He leaned against the wall as she pulled on her shoes. "Do you have any idea how beautiful you are to me?"

"No. I mean, you say it a lot to me, but I have a hard time equating the person you think I am to myself." He came toward her. "If you touch me now, we'll never find out what happened out there, and I really want to know."

As they made their way downstairs, she turned to the kitchen before heading to the living room. Once there, she felt her belly growl, and before she could say anything to Daniel, he handed her two thick roast beef sandwiches and a large glass of tea. She was munching on one of them when she entered the living room.

"I see you're feeling pretty good. And hungry. Joey said that as a magical being, you'll burn more calories." Coleen nodded at Chris. "Boy, that looks really good. Can I have Daniel make me one?"

"Here, take this one. I think if I eat both of these I might need another nap." The two of them shared the sandwiches while the men talked about Vegas. When they were done, Coleen felt almost…well, she felt almost human again.

After they were told what they'd found out by going to Vegas rather than just using the phone, she tried to think what this would mean for her now. Her belly started to churn up and her head was spinning when Chris touched her hand to hers and told her she was fine.

"So I don't owe them all that money?" Joey told her that she not only didn't owe them money, but that there was going to be a lawsuit brought against them and the firm that they'd worked for, and she might be getting part of the bigger picture. "I don't want anything from them. I mean, at least I hadn't paid them anything yet. Think of all the other people that they hurt. They more than likely could use it more than me."

"True, and they will get a part as well. Most of the money that was in accounts all over the world is now in the hands of some people who are going to make sure that it's given to the right people. And Coleen, there is a lot of ill-gotten gains from this firm. All told, there were nineteen people in on it, and a few more that they're still looking for. William Taylor—he helped us get things going out there—is putting together a task force that will gather all the information that we found at the offices and their homes, and make sure that the money is returned to everyone that paid in; and failing that, the families of their victims." Coleen asked how that was different. "Because as they pointed out, some people worked themselves to death to pay it back, or some simply lost everything, as you did, to make it right. The money that was paid to them through these fake billings, it will be paid back too as soon as they have a good accounting of it all. On your behalf, we sued for duress as well as the money you lost on the sale of your home. Also, you will get your money back on the funeral costs that you paid. What you're going to get is coming from their estates, the company, and any holdings that they have. You brought the two of them to light. William thinks that if they're made an example of, other attorneys will think twice before trying this again. They're going away for a very long time."

No one knew how much the men were worth. Chris had an idea, she told her, but not all the information was in just yet. Coleen understood that, she told her, but she was still not really sure why she'd get money.

"I just want it off my records, and to not have to worry about this money all the time. I mean, I was never going to be able to pay it all back. I can see that now. They had me on the hook, and they were going to try and drain me dry." Joey said that was why it was important for him to do this for her. "Thank you, but really, all I want is to know that it wasn't anything that Micky did. He wasn't...he wasn't right in the head about things, I know, but I didn't think he'd do something like this."

"You were wronged, Coleen, both of you were. You had to sell your home, everything that you owned, as well as take care of your ex-husband's funeral immediately, instead of paying it off a bit at a time as was a normal way of doing it. Not to mention, had the funeral home not been informed that you were not divorced from Greer, you would never have been told to pay the bill at all. You should know that the arrangements that you paid for, the lobster and steak thing? That was all contrived as well. And the paperwork at the courthouse, it was there, filed under a different number than you were given when you asked for copies. They played you from the very beginning. Everyone that was involved, from the hospital to the attorneys that hurt you, has to pay." She looked at Tony when Chris finished speaking. Had they not done this to her, she would never have met him. It was a winner for her all around. Chris laughed. "Yes, I love the way your mind is thinking. And it's time we left."

They were gone within five minutes. When she looked at Tony and asked him if it had been something she'd said, he only laughed. Then he took her to his office to show her something.

"The Times ran the article about Bentley's the day after the critic left Ohio. When I spoke to Micah about it, he said that it usually took a week or so, but they were really impressed and ran it in the next edition." She asked him what it said. "I don't know. I wanted to read it with you."

"Really?" He said yes and picked her up and put her on his lap while they tried to find the page in the stack of newspapers that were on his desk. "This is going to be bad, I just know it. I mean, why would they run something that is just so-so? He must have really panned me badly. I hope that he doesn't mention Tansy or Matt. This could hurt their chances of getting in with someone good."

"I think they're in with someone good, love. You're going to take very good care of them." He looked at her before reading. "'I had the most amazing dinner tonight. Thankfully my wife and I had engine trouble as we were returning home from a long and arduous trip. I was exhausted and hungry, and found this beautiful little hole in the wall restaurant still serving. They were actually closed, as we were told upon entering, but we were seated when the cook said she'd serve us what she had. And what a delightful treat she was as well.'"

"That can't be right. Who are you reading about?" He read the headline to her again. "He said he got a treat. All we served him was what was on the menu."

"Hush. Where was I? Oh, here. 'What a delightful treat she

was as well. After having Cornish hen with the most amazing sauce over it, we also had a pork tenderloin with a peach glaze sauce. Grilled peaches were served up as well, and the fresh gnocchi and vegetables were perfection. My wife, not usually a fan of fish, nearly ate all of the grilled trout on her own, and only shared a few bites when I traded her for the hen. Every morsel of this meal was delicious. And then they brought out the dessert.

"'I will say that should I ever find myself in this little town in Ohio again, I will beg to be allowed entrance to Ms. Bentley's fine table. The staff was attentive without being annoying or noisy. The dining room, as I have said, was closed, but there was no feeling of being rushed out the door because we were the last people there. And even when the chef herself came out to meet us, she was kind, quiet, and praised her staff working with her as if she'd had very little to do with our meal, when we know for a fact that she was the one that cooked it. I am to understand that she has two wonderful under chefs in Tansy Miller and Matt James, and I can only hope that these two learn not just cooking skills from this woman, but all manner of things in running the best five-star restaurant that I've been to in more years than I can think of.'"

Coleen looked at Tony, waiting for him to say, "Just kidding." Five stars? There was no way that she'd gotten five-stars. Taking the paper from him, she scanned the article again, seeing the key words that she'd heard before getting to the last lines, just before the address, email address, as well as phone number for reservations.

"Did you have this printed up to make me feel better?"

Tony shook his head. "Then you had one of the others do it. As a joke. I think it's really funny, don't you?"

"It's not a joke, love." She nodded and he shook his head. "No, this is the real deal. You were awarded a five-star rating by one of the biggest critics in the world. But I have to tell you, I'm not the least bit surprised. I think he should have given you ten. At least."

She stood up and dropped the paper on the floor. Her mind kept going over each point in her head. Delightful. Fine table. Amazing dinner. Delicious. Coleen looked at Tony and felt pressured, her body too tight. She heard him calling her name, but suddenly she felt different.

~~~

Tony looked at his mate as her panther. Christ, she was beautiful, and afraid. He moved slowly toward her, talking softly so as not to startle her again, and made his way to the back doors of the office.

"You're beautiful. I'd take your picture, but I left my cell up...here it is." He took several pictures of her as she moved around the room, sure that the house had provided his phone for him. "When we get back, I'm going to show them to you. But for now, I'm going to open the door to the yard. Just be careful where you go, and remember that walking on four feet is different than walking on two."

Her cat moved toward him, watching each of her paws as she set them down. He knew she was being careful of her steps, but he wanted to see her run, her fur laying back on her flesh as she jumped and rolled in the grass. Even the snow flying up from around her when she played outdoors. As she was

Anthony

rubbing her fur over his legs, Tony felt his cock stretch and thicken at the thought of taking her now, his cat enjoying his mate as much as Tony did her human part. When she made her way out to the deck, he followed and snapped a dozen more pictures when she walked into the snow-covered yard.

Taking off his shirt after setting his phone back on the desk, Tony kept an eye on her. She was running around jumping over every little thing. She looked and acted like a kitten with a ball of yarn. He smiled at her as she enjoyed herself. Twice she fell, but rolled with it and got back up, only to go back and leap again. Tony was still laughing when he let his cat take him.

He took his time going after her. They had all the time in the world to be together, and he was going to enjoy this first time as much as he could. Following her scent, he could see that he was going to have to give her lessons in being sneaky, but thought for now at least, he'd be able to keep her in his sights. Just as he came up behind her, she turned and looked at him. It was then that he noticed that one of her eyes was as dark as his, the other as blue as hers had been.

You're beautiful. She moved along his body, rubbing her scent over his cat. When she was finished, he did the same, his cat nipping at her twice when she moved away. Standing behind her, he moved up over her body and pressed her shoulders to the ground. When she started to pull out from under him, his cat sank his teeth into her shoulder. *Let him have you. He needs his mate.*

He's a brute. Tony laughed and felt his cat's approval. *I need you. Please. I really need you.*

He fucked her hard, taking her to the ground over and

over until his cat had had his pleasure. Tony had heard that the female seldom got much out of this kind of coupling. He figured that was why they fought so hard when the female was dominated by the male. When he backed from her, Coleen turned around and snapped her teeth at his cat, making him back away from her.

He thought that his cat would be pissed, but again, he was proud of his mate. When she shifted into her human self, his cat moved between her legs to have his fill of her before Tony could. And when she screamed out his name, holding onto his fur, Tony fell in love with her all over again.

She came twice, begging him for more. It was all he could do not to toss her back to the ground and feast on her again. And when it was his turn, he didn't move from where his cat had been, and ate Coleen with long lapping strokes that give him what he wanted and had her coming again and again. Moving up her body, his cock in his fist, Tony knew that he could take her as hard as he wanted and she'd love it. With her being a cat now, he'd not have to hold back. Tony felt his cock thicken even more at that thought. Slamming forward into her entrance, he took her mouth as he had her pussy, and fucked her with his tongue. Coleen held onto him with her feet wrapped around his legs as she took everything that he gave her.

Her nails dug deep into his back, her breasts tightened and swelled under his touch. Taking one of the heavy morsels into his mouth, he bit down hard enough to draw blood, and nursed from her while he felt his balls fill, his cock hardening even more. And when she threw back her head, her body bowing up off the ground, he licked her throat and took her pounding

194

Anthony

pulse into his mouth. Then he bit her there as well, bringing not just her over, but himself as well.

Pulling from her, he flipped her to her belly and lifted her ass up. His need was pounding at him; the need to dominate, to take and mark, made him thoughtless to her needs. He was buried deep within her pussy before she could pull away. Fucking her this way, he reached under her and tugged hard at her nipple until he was full again.

"Come for me." She told him no, she wasn't ready, that she needed more. Sliding to her pussy, he pressed his thumb over her clit then pinched it, ordering her to come again. Her scream tore through the woods, making not just the birds fly off, but he heard some of the larger animals scatter as well. Tony bit into her shoulder as his cock emptied once more.

The feeling of being complete washed over him, making him weak with his releases. Leaning over her, holding himself and her up from the cold ground, he tried to control not just his pounding heart but his breathing as well. He was drained; never had he felt this way after sex.

When he thought he could move, he held her body to his and rolled to his back. As she moved around so that she was laying over him, he held her close and trailed his fingers up and down her back. Christ, he was in love with her was all he could think about.

"I love you." He looked at her when she spoke, her voice soft. He told her that he loved her as well. "It was hard to come to love you, I know that, but you've changed my life; not just by being a cat, but changed everything about my personal self and gave me worth. I wonder now why I fought it so hard."

195

"You'd been hurt. And you didn't trust. I understand that." He held her as the birds overhead started to come back to their roosts. "Joey told me that once things start to come out about that firm, there will be a lot of questions about every case they tried. Even ones that were in litigation. He said that he was glad that someone from the state department has stepped in to make sure things aren't too bad. But I do think about the ones that were had by these men. And had it not been for you coming here, they would have kept going and going."

"It's going to be nice not having that amount of money hanging over my head, I will admit that. I was having nightmares about someone coming out to the restaurant and taking it from me." He asked her if that was why she'd never taken the building from his grandda. "Mostly. I mean, someone would surely try and take a piece of it if they had any idea that I was the owner of the place, don't you think?"

"I do, yes. You're a very smart cookie. I guess that's another reason I love you so much." She laughed and shivered. "I guess we should go inside. But it's so peaceful out here. Once summer hits, these woods will be full of young animals, as well as the noises that go along with them. And with Pip's adventure too, the flowers that she's planting for the faerie queen, this place will be alive with all sorts of creatures."

"I think I could get used to this, the nature so close to where we live. In the city you don't have this kind of green and things blooming like you do here. And nothing like this in Vegas. It's noisy, then nothing for miles and miles." He told her about the things that Chris had purchased, and how much fun she'd had being where there were shops and theaters. "She'd never

196

survive out there for very long. She likes the woods and earth too much."

When they both got up, they made their way back to the house. They were in the office again when he showed her the pictures of her cat, and she remarked on how her eyes were so different. He had no idea why they had done that.

"I'll ask Micah. Or my grandparents. I personally think it's beautiful, but there might be some sort of reason for it." He pulled her into his arms when she was dressed. "What would I have done had you not come into my life?"

"Been as lonely as I would have been."

He agreed. There wasn't any other way for him to have ever been this happy.

When Daniel was serving them a late lunch, Coleen's phone went off. When she ignored it, the kitchen phone rang, then his cell. He knew that it wasn't his family; had it been, they would have contacted him. But when he picked up his phone, he had to smile. Tansy sounded frantic.

"Did you know that we're getting calls off the hook? I can't clean out the walk-in and take an.... The phone will not stop ringing. I've taken as many.... Can you have Coleen call me? It's really, really important." He handed the phone to Coleen.

Tony had an idea that they were busy because of the article. And there was no telling how many calls they might have gotten that no one had answered since it came out. He knew that Tansy, as well as a couple of others, had gone into Bentley's to work today. No one, as far as he knew, had been there since they'd closed up on Saturday night. When he cleared the plates in front of her, he leaned back in his chair to watch her.

"I can have a calendar put on one of those pad thingies. I don't have one so...I don't even know where to get one." He raised his hand. "Okay, Tony can get it for us. Just...I have no idea. Just let it ring for now, and when I come in we'll sort it out. Are you sure that they have the right number?"

Tony heard Tansy laugh. Tony was pretty sure that this was only the beginning, and that the family would be lucky if they were ever able to get a table again. He looked at Daniel, who was smiling like a loon.

"She's famous. I had to be really careful of not saying what I'd read about the new place when I was feeding you, but boy, oh boy, I am just as proud as can be." Tony noticed that one of the faeries was on Daniel's shoulder as he made his way around the kitchen, and he asked the big man about it. "We're friends. Awnia and Gom, they just come and go now that I understand to leave them a space open in the window and such. Just yesterday they helped me put together some flower arrangements in the front hall. I just shoved them in the vase, and she had me moving them here and there. Looked really good when we were done, if I do say so myself."

When Coleen got off the phone, she looked tense. He asked her if she was all right. After a short harsh laugh, she got up and entered the pantry. When she came out, he could see that she was going to cook. Daniel simply slipped out of the room and Tony stayed where he was.

"She said that people are booking for months from now. Tansy told one man that they didn't have any seating on the night in question, and he begged her for a table outside. When she explained to him that we didn't have outdoor seating, he told her that he'd pay for it to be put in and that he'd be the first to have a seat. I don't even want to think about the Christmas reservations she's taken…a few of them big parties, too." He said nothing as she put things in the mixer. There wasn't a single measuring cup or spoon used, but he'd bet that it was dead on for what she needed. When she turned to look at him he could see panic in her eyes. "What am I going to do?"

"All right, if I tell you, will you tell me what you're making?" She nodded and said it was bread. "Okay, Chris and Joey are going to talk to the rest of the family, and they're going to pay for you to expand."

"I can't expand. I don't have the money, nor do I want to go into debt right now to do it. And if you tell me they want to pay for it, I have to tell them no." He asked her why not. "Because it's a great deal of money on something that might not work."

"Did I tell you how much we're worth? Not just you and I, but my family?" She shook her head and continued putting flour in the mixer's bowl. "Billions. You and I are worth billions. And even if we weren't very wealthy, my entire family is. Especially Joey and Chris. A very old and very rich vampire left money to Joey, and he had plenty before."

"It's their money. And did you say…billions?" He said he had. "I'll deal with that later; my mind can't take too much more of thinking of how many zeros that is. But aside from that, what if next week people realize what a major flop I am? And suddenly no one wants to eat there. Can you hand me the milk?"

He got up and got the milk out of the fridge, as well as the cranberries and oranges she wanted. He wondered how that was going to go into the bread, but said nothing. She was working on her stress level; he didn't want to add to it.

"You're going to be successful for a very long time, love. I know that as well as anyone that has the pleasure of eating anything that you cook." She dumped what looked to him like three cups of cranberries in the batter, along with a bunch of chopped nuts. Whatever she was making, he was going to have to hide it from Grandda when he came over. "How about we go ahead with the expansion, just you and I, and even put in a patio that some people can eat at when they come for dinner?"

"I'd have to hire more staff." He nodded and sat down with a pad of paper and a pen. "The kitchen will need to be bigger too. I don't mean just for the extra hands that will be needed, but a bigger grill and oven area. And the walk-in too. And the dining area alone will need more space, along with the tables and chairs. Then there is the added expense of all the cutlery and glasses. Christ, it's too much."

"Plates and silverware as well as glasses; got it." She nodded and poured the mixture out on the large island to knead. "Do you plan to make your own bread too? While I have no idea what that is you're making, I cannot wait to have some of it."

"It's going to be fruit bread. I have no idea if it'll be any good, but I have to do.... We can't expand." He felt the disappointment all the way to his feet. "The building next to Bentley's...do you know who owns it? I'm assuming your grandda does. And would he be willing to sell it?"

"Are you thinking of moving into that building?" She told him that she could see expanding sideways instead of back. "Oh, I can see that. And there is a second floor there that you can use for larger parties."

"I don't know about the patio idea. That would mean tables need to be bug free, as well as something that won't get too hot to sit on in the evening. And it would only be in use for a few months out of the year." He nodded, knowing that none of that would be a problem for people who really wanted to eat there. "This is going to be costly, Tony. Like hundreds of thousands of dollars expensive. And that's not even taking into account the cost of the building."

"You and I own the building, so that's not going to be an issue. It came with the offices that I bought. You know as well as I do that the moment you start expanding, the magic will help where it can." She nodded as she took her stress out on the dough. "You can do this, love. I know you can."

"And if I fail, are you going to be there to pick up the pieces? Because as nervous as I am about this, I'm just as terrified." He got up and wrapped his arms around her waist. "I love you."

"I love you as well. And you will never have to worry about me not being there to pick up the pieces or to cheer you on. I will be here for you however you need me." He kissed her neck. "But I want to be paid for being the host from now on."

"Deal."

Tony sat down and watched her. He knew that she'd never be secure in what she did, even though all those around her could see it. But he'd also bet that no matter what, she'd give everything all that she had, and that would make her a success.

CHAPTER 13

Carol heard someone coming down the hall, and she was nearly to the point of begging someone to let her go. The walls were closing in on her, and no matter how many blankets they brought her, she could not get warm. She told one of the officers that she was going to sue him for trying to kill her with the cold.

"It's wintertime. It's supposed to be cold this time of year. We have no control over the weather." He had handed her another blanket. "There is no more of those either. I asked the captain, and he said that for every one you use, I have to wash it up myself. So, that's all you get." She told him that it was his job to make sure she was comfortable. "Yeah, comfortable, but not costing me extra work. You'll make do."

And she had been trying that since yesterday. And no matter how many times she told them, no one would get her any kind of electric blanket either. Fuckers. They were all going to pay. She turned to look at the woman standing at her cell.

"What do you want?" She wanted nothing to do with these people, and less to do with Coleen. "Unless you have a key to

203

get me out of here, then go the fuck away."

"Always such a pleasure to talk to you. But I came to inform you of a few things before you go to court this afternoon. It could go better for you if you listen to me." Carol told her to go away. "Suit yourself. But I'm thinking that you won't like prison any more than you do here."

"Wait." Coleen stopped walking away but didn't come back. "You tell me whatever it is you think you need to, then I'll tell you want I want. That way we both get to be disappointed."

"I'm not going to be disappointed in anything that you do or don't do. As of the moment that you tried to take Mandy and kidnap her, we were finished." Carol stood up and tried to tell her, again, that it wasn't kidnapping. "Will you admit to trying to take her and say it was a mistake?"

"Mistake? For what? I have been trying to tell you for the last week, I wasn't trying to kidnap her. I just wanted her to come with me until I got the money that your fucking brother owes me." Coleen just shook her head and walked away. "Come back here. I said to get your ass back here."

The door closed and Carol sat down. She'd been given a dress to put on; it looked like Bethany had picked it out. The color was just plain ugly, and there wasn't even a nice pair of new shoes to go with it. Carol had some sense of style, and it wasn't those sack dresses that Bethany wore.

An hour later, after refusing to put the rag on, she was taken by car to the courthouse. It was just as drab and old as the jail was. Not that she cared all that much. Carol figured after today that she'd be going home, and she'd have to think of another way to get some money from them. Maybe she'd go and see about bringing Sheppard's in-laws to her house. Somebody would surely pay to get them back.

The room wasn't full, which was fine by her. Coleen was there with her husband, as well as a group of people sitting at the table with Sheppard. Carol didn't see Mandy, and figured they were keeping her away in the event she tried to take her home with her again. It had been her plan, but they'd fucked that up as well.

"Ms. Lewis, you have been charged with attempted kidnapping, attempted blackmail, and—"

"I did not try to kidnap that kid. For Christ's sake, will you fuckers get over that shit? I was only going to take her to my house until her daddy saw reason and paid me. He had them government people take my income away when there wasn't any reason for it whatsoever. Do you have any idea how much of a pain in the ass one kid can be?" He asked her to clean up her language. "Clean it up? Damn it, I'm an old woman who knows her mind. Get over yourself."

"By the very definition of the word kidnapping, that is exactly what you said you were doing. Let me read it to you here." When she started to tell him to fuck off again, he looked at her over his glasses and she shut up. Christ, this was the dumbest thing she'd ever been caught up in. "To kidnap is to seize and hold a person, or in this case a child, against that person's will by force or fraud. Often for a ransom. And in the event you think what you were asking for wasn't ransom either, let me tell you that it is. The redeeming or release of a captive—again, the child of Sheppard Spencer—by paying money or complying with other demands. So, Ms. Lewis, were you or were you not kidnapping the minor child of your nephew?"

"She was going to come to my house for a bit. He owes me money. I don't know how the hell you all got kidnapping out of that, but I guess there is no telling you fuckers right from wrong when you get something stuck in your head." He asked her again to curb her language. "Look, don't you think this shit has gone on long enough? Christ, I just wanted to get what was mine. He should never have had that bitch go in and take money out of my account. I had plans for that money. And not only am I broke, but there ain't no more coming in either. How fair is that?"

"I would say very fair. You don't have the child, thank goodness. You aren't caring for her, again, thankfully. And as far as I can see, you don't even like her. Right?" She told him that she hated the very ground she walked on. "See? You're ahead of the game because you don't have her. Now. On this other matter of you spitting on one of the officers that arrested you. You do know that—"

"Wait. Wait. Wait. I'm not done yet. How the hell am I supposed to get my money? You never said." He asked her what money. "The money that he owes me. I don't think you should just fucking gloss over that like it wasn't anything. I told you, I need that money."

"There is not going to be any money given to you, Ms. Lewis. There is no reason whatsoever for you to think that there might be. You were in the wrong, and unless you drop this foolishness, you'll be held in jail until you see reason. You're just lucky that they're willing to drop the charges of kidnapping if you promise to just go away." She stood up and the man sitting next to her told her to sit down and shut up. "Ms. Lewis, you are trying my patience."

"Good, at least I know you're not fucking dead from the neck up. Mother fuck, this is just stupid. Sheppard has money now…I saw his gun and shit. I have expenses, and he needs to put the money back in my account so I can pay my shit off." He leaned back in his big seat. "There ain't no reason that he can't give me money every month. Say a couple of grand. That would keep me from having to come up here and taking Mandy back to have him pay up."

"You mean that even though I've explained to you that you are kidnapping her when you try to take her, you'd do it again to get Mr. Spencer to pay you?" She nodded, thankful that the dumbass was finally getting it. "You know, I don't think I've ever had anyone be so blatant about what their kidnapping plans were. You really have no concept of what the consequences of your confessions are, do you?"

"If you mean I take her and he pays me, yeah, I understand that. He shouldn't have been allowed to take the money back anyway." He asked her why she felt entitled to it. "Well, it's not like the government cares one diddle who has her. I don't care to have her either, but I will take her back with me if I can't get him to see reason. And when the hell has the government ever moved fast on shit like this? I mean, Christ, it took them almost two months for me to get my welfare card in the mail. That money has been real nice too, but since he stuck his nose in my business, I don't even get that anymore."

"No, you won't. Fraud is frowned upon." He looked over at Sheppard and she did too. Carol hated him almost as much as she did his sister. "Mr. Spencer, I don't see this ending any way but her continuing to try and kidnap your daughter, do you?"

"No sir." She screamed at them both that it wasn't fucking kidnapping. "Sir, if you would just take my prior conditions off the table, you can do with her as you see fit. I have talked to the people that she owes a great deal of gambling debt to and convinced them that I am not responsible for her bills, and believe that has been taken care of. If you send her home, I think they might want a few words with her as well."

"What the fuck do you mean, you've been talking to the people I owe money too? They said they'd get it from you one way or another. You ain't gonna pay that either? Mother fuck, what good are you anyway?" She looked at the judge. "I'm telling you right now, if you send me home, I'm going to be coming back here to get her. Fuck that shit. I want you to make him take care of me. He owes me."

"So you keep saying." He picked up the file and looked to be reading it over. She wondered if he could even read at all. He was more than likely just reading one of them dirty books. When he put it down, she noticed a smile. Finally, things were about to look up. "Ms. Lewis, it is with great pleasure that I remand you over to trial. Not just for the attempted kidnapping charges, but for.... Well, let's just say you're going to need a good lawyer."

Even as she was being pulled away, she was screaming at them all. Sheppard was going to pay her even if she had to fucking hold him at gunpoint. This was just the dumbest thing she'd ever been witness too. And when they put her in the back of the big van again, she noticed that her blankets were gone as well.

"Hey, you need to get me somewhere I can get a blanket or two that ain't so thin I can read through it." Nothing. "Did you fucking hear me? I said that I'm cold back here, and you need to get me something warm to wrap up in. I won't be suffering because of some cock sucking judge who doesn't know the difference between kidnapping and other shit."

When she was returned to her cell, her blankets there were gone too, and the one on her bed was thinner than any of the others she'd been brought. Yelling at them to find her more, she was ignored. This was just fucking stupid. They were all mother fuckers, every fucking one of them.

Sitting on the bed to try to figure out what to do now, she noticed that the floor seemed to move. It took her a moment to realize that it was covered in bugs, millions of them. Carol put her feet up on the bed and screamed for help.

"Shut up." Carol felt her teeth snap together when one of them spoke to her. "You are a bad person."

"I am not. What the fuck are you?" The little dark bug moved up to her bed and stood beside her. "You're a person. What the hell? A little tiny person."

"I'm a faerie. And as I said, you are a bad person. While we're not to kill you, we can try to convince you that you must confess to the courts what you have done, and then we will go away." Carol just laughed. "You will not think it so funny if we were to scare you enough that you confess."

"Bring it on, bitch. I'm not afraid of a little shit like you." She reached out to flick her away when she moved, bright wings lifting her from the bed to be in front of Carol's face. "What the hell are you?"

"I've told you. Faerie." She flew around her head so many times that Carol stopped trying to keep up with her. "You have no redeeming qualities, not a single one. I think that you will have to go."

"Good. You get me out of here and I'll pay you. I want to get that kid too; do you know how to do that?" The thing told her that she wasn't to touch young Mandy. "Oh yeah? Well fuck you. I'm going to get her, take her home with me, and then we'll see how quickly he pays up. He owes me."

~~~

Dark reached out to the witch queen, as well as her own lady. *I think there's no hope for her, my ladies. She is without thought to how her actions affect those around her. I think she is set on this task that she has thought of, and will not quit it.*

You have searched her deeply, my lady Dark? You know her mind as well as your own? She told her queen that she had, and yes, Carol would not stop until she was dead or the child was taken. *What will become of the child Mandy should she take her this time?*

She will die. The witch queen asked her if she was sure. *I am, my lady. I have the ability of seeing the future. It is both a gift and a curse. But should she be allowed to leave here, even if only to go home, the child Mandy will know no peace other than in death. This woman will kill her in a fit of rage, and hurt many others in her wake.*

Then you know what to do. Dark told her that she would do it, that she had her army with her now. The witch queen told her to come to her when she was finished.

You will end my life, my lady? The witch asked her why she'd think that. *I have only done what was necessary to keep your family safe, a promise that I made long ago to Lady Myra. You know as well as I that her death, even the way we will have to do it, will not go well with the others. Lady Coleen will be hurt, Master Sheppard will feel it is his fault, and the rest, her sister included, will feel a pain in their hearts deeply, even though they had no love for her.*

Can you make it…natural looking? Dark looked at the woman on the bed, who was currently trying to smash the men that had come with her. But they were quick and not without their own magic. *Do you think you could do that?*

Yes, my lady. We have worked this magic before. The witch again told her to come see her when she was finished. *I will be there.*

With a heavy heart, knowing that the witch was going to have her put to death, Dark reached out to her men. They were to terrify the woman, make her think she was under attack.

But leave no marks if you can help it. We do not want anyone to think she died for any other reason than because she was old and of poor health.

With a short nod to them, it began. They swarmed her over and over, never purposefully touching her, but coming close. They did get tangled in her hair a couple of times, and her smacking out at them had them tumbling over and over. Within minutes of the order, the woman fell back on the floor, dead. Her blackness, which others thought of as a heart, beat no more.

Dark dismissed her army. They were plentiful, and she made sure that they stayed close should she need them. As she made her way to the witch queen, she let her own Lady Aurora know that the woman was dead.

You have done the family a great service, my Dark Bloom. As you have always done in serving me. She asked her if her death would be quick. *Your death? The witch queen has no desire to kill you, Dark. She wishes to reward you for your help in this.*

You are sure? Lady Aurora laughed. *I thought her to end my life, and my service to you.*

Nay, you will see when you go to her. She is a good person, and will wish you only the best. This I promise you.

Dark arrived and knelt before the queen. It was hard to not beg for her life, even though she had been told that her death wasn't going to happen.

"Rise up, my friend." Dark rose to be even with her, face to face. "Nolan told me that you helped him once, by killing a monster that was going to hurt his children. I owe you a great deal."

"He was going to kill again." The queen nodded and asked her to have a seat. Dark landed on the small table next to her and asked her why she was there.

"Aurora said that you have a single desire in your life. I wish to grant you that wish." Dark felt her heart pound in her chest. She wanted to beg her to say it, to tell her that she was going to really do this for her. "Would you still like the wish granted?"

"I...? What would...? This will come at what cost, my lady?" The witch asked her what she meant. "Would I no longer be a faerie? My magic, it means so much to me. So does this thing I desire, but should I not be able to be magical, I'm not sure what I could do in this world."

212

"You will lose nothing." Dark nodded, still not sure that there wasn't a catch. "Would you like for me to grant you this wish?"

Dark looked at the house that the woman had; the riches that were before her that Dark knew she saw. Others might not, but the witch did. Dark looked at her then, wondering if by saying yes, she was making the biggest mistake of her life. But she had wanted this since she was nothing but a speck.

"I would, my lady. Very much so." With a nod, Dark felt the magic take her. Her body twisted, her head spun quickly. As she morphed, changed and grew, she could feel her magic as it took the pain from her, how it filled her completely, even with the changes to her body. And when she fell to her knees, breaking the small table that she'd been standing on, Dark stood up and looked at the witch queen. "I am a person."

"Yes. You're a very lovely person too." With a nod from the queen, Dark turned. There behind her was a large mirror. Walking to it, she looked at the creature staring back at her. "You are very lovely, Dark Bloom. Welcome to this world."

Before You Go...

HELP AN AUTHOR

write a review

THANK YOU!

Share your voice and help guide other readers to these wonderful books. Even if it's only a line or two your reviews help readers discover the author's books so they can continue creating stories that you'll love. Login to your favorite retailer and leave a review. Thank you.

AWARD WINNING, BESTSELLING AUTHOR

Kathi Barton, winner of the Pinnacle Book Achievement award as well as a best-selling author on Amazon and All Romance books, lives in Nashport, Ohio with her husband Paul. When not creating new worlds and romance, Kathi and her husband enjoy camping and going to auctions. She can also be seen at county fairs with her husband who is an artist and potter.

Her muse, a cross between Jimmy Stewart and Hugh Jackman, brings her stories to life for her readers in a way that has them coming back time and again for more. Her favorite genre is paranormal romance with a great deal of spice. You can visit Kathi online and drop her an email if you'd like. She loves hearing from her fans. aaronskiss@gmail.com.

Follow Kathi on her blog: http://kathisbartonauthor.blogspot.com/

www.ingramcontent.com/pod-product-compliance
Lightning Source LLC
Chambersburg PA
CBHW021957190626
46808CB00017B/2052